Echoes of the Abyss - Shadows of Control towards Chasing Normal

Jessica Hintz

Published by Jessica Hintz, 2024.

This is a work of fiction. Similarities to real people, places, or events are entirely coincidental.

ECHOES OF THE ABYSS - SHADOWS OF CONTROL TOWARDS CHASING NORMAL

First edition. October 23, 2024.

Copyright © 2024 Jessica Hintz.

ISBN: 979-8227782014

Written by Jessica Hintz.

Echoes of the Abyss
Shadows of Control towards Chasing Normal

Jessica hintz

United States
2024

Imprint

Book Title: Echoes of the Abyss - Shadows of Control towards Chasing Normal
Author: Jessica Hintz
© 2024, Jessica Hintz
All rights reserved.
Author: Jessica Hintz
Contact: boxingboy898337@gmail.com

Chapter 1: Whispers in the Dark

I have never heard silence this loud.

Even the faintest echo of my breath, the subtle creak of the floor beneath my feet—it all reverberates through the emptiness around me, like the walls themselves are listening, waiting. The thin, pale beams of light slicing through the gaps in the blinds cast eerie shadows that flicker like whispers. It's enough to make you wonder if the room is alive, if it's thinking and watching as much as I am.

But maybe that's just me.

They tell me I'm unwell, broken, twisted somehow. It's a joke, really. I've seen the doctors, the shrinks, the hollow faces behind clipboards and questions, but none of them understand. They try to pick at my brain, probing, dissecting every thought. They think they can fit me into some neat little box, slap a label on it, and call it a day. But I know better.

Because I'm not broken. I'm free.

I never believed them, not when they took me in, and certainly not now. Even here, in this place they call an "institution," I'm more awake than I've ever been. The walls around me may be padded, the doors locked, but the real prison has always been out there—in the world they call normal.

I walk slowly toward the window, feeling the coldness of the floor seep through my bare feet. Outside, the streetlights flicker, casting a dim glow across the city that stretches beyond my reach. It's almost beautiful, in a distant, untouchable way, but there's something about it that disgusts me. The people out there, walking the streets like mindless drones, going about their lives as if they're in control. They have no idea how fragile it all is.

I laugh to myself. Control—what a lie.

Control is nothing but an illusion, a story they tell themselves so they don't have to face the truth. But the truth... the truth is that chaos lurks beneath every carefully crafted lie, waiting for the right moment to tear through the fabric of their precious lives. I've seen it. I've felt it. I've *been* it.

But they don't want to know about that. No, they'd rather lock me away, keep me in here so they don't have to face what they can't understand. I'm a threat to them, a reminder of the darkness they pretend doesn't exist. That's why they brought me here, to this silent, empty place where the walls are my only company.

It wasn't always like this. Once upon a time, I walked among them, blending in, pretending to care, pretending to feel what they felt. But pretending can only get you so far before the mask starts to crack.

It cracked for me when I was fourteen.

I didn't even feel anything when it happened. That's what they don't understand—there was no rush of adrenaline, no wave of guilt. Just a calm, quiet moment. A release. It was a choice, pure and simple. A way to set things right. They call me a monster for it, but I know the truth. What I did wasn't wrong. It was necessary.

The doctors tell me that my condition is called "antisocial personality disorder." A fancy way of saying I don't fit into their world. I've heard them use other terms too—sociopath, psychopath. The labels don't matter. They've been trying to fix me ever since. Medication. Therapy. Endless questions about how I feel. The irony is that they don't really care how I feel. They care about making me fit into their idea of normal.

Normal.

The word makes my skin crawl. It's something they want me to chase, something they dangle in front of me like a carrot, as if it's a prize

I should be striving for. But I don't want their normal. I don't want to fit into their world of rules and masks. I want to be free—truly free.

I can't help but wonder, as I stand by the window, how long it will take them to realize that they can't fix me. How long before they give up and accept the fact that I don't belong in their carefully ordered universe? It doesn't matter, really. I'll leave this place eventually, one way or another. Until then, I wait. I listen. I plan.

The sound of footsteps in the hallway pulls me from my thoughts. I turn my head slightly, just enough to catch the faint shuffle of shoes against the tile floor. They're coming for me again. Another session with Dr. Hayes, another round of questions, another attempt to break through the walls I've built around myself.

I smile.

They think they're the ones in control, but I'm the one who holds the power. I decide what they see, what they hear, what they believe. They don't know it, but they're part of my game now, and I'm always three moves ahead.

The door clicks open, and in steps Dr. Hayes, clipboard in hand, his face a mask of calm professionalism. He's older than most of the staff here, with graying hair and wire-rimmed glasses that he adjusts nervously every time I look at him too long. He's afraid of me, though he'd never admit it. I can see it in the way his eyes flicker when I speak, in the way he shifts in his seat when I tell him what he wants to hear.

"Good morning, Elise," he says, his voice carefully measured.

Elise. That's the name they gave me here. It's not my real name, of course. My real name doesn't matter anymore. Here, I am whoever they want me to be.

"Good morning, Doctor," I reply, my voice sweet and soft, like honey dripping from a blade.

He sits down across from me, flipping through his notes. "How are you feeling today?"

The same question, every time. It's almost amusing how predictable they are. But I play along, because that's what I do. I play their game until they don't even realize they're losing.

"I'm feeling... better," I say, letting just the slightest hint of vulnerability slip into my voice. "I think I'm starting to understand things more clearly now."

His pen pauses, just for a moment, before he jots something down. He glances up at me, his eyes searching for the lie. But he won't find it, not in the way he's looking.

"That's good to hear," he says. "Progress is important."

Progress. Another lie.

"What have you been thinking about?" he asks, leaning forward slightly. "Anything you'd like to share?"

I tilt my head, letting a slow smile spread across my lips. "I've been thinking about control."

His eyes flicker, and I know I've got him. He doesn't say anything, just waits for me to continue, like the good little doctor he is.

"Control is funny, don't you think?" I say, my voice soft and steady. "Everyone thinks they have it, but no one really does. It's like sand slipping through your fingers—no matter how tightly you try to hold on, it always gets away."

He nods slowly, his pen hovering over the paper, ready to capture whatever insight he thinks I'm about to reveal. I almost laugh. He doesn't understand that the only insight here is the one I want him to see.

"Do you feel like you're losing control?" he asks, his voice careful, cautious.

I shrug. "Maybe. Or maybe I'm gaining it. It's hard to tell, isn't it? Sometimes, losing control is the only way to really be free."

His pen scribbles furiously, and I watch him, amused by how seriously he takes this. He thinks he's peeling back layers, getting closer to the truth. But the truth is something he'll never touch.

"Do you want to be free, Elise?" he asks, his eyes narrowing slightly as if he's testing me.

I meet his gaze, letting my smile fade. "Don't you?"

He doesn't answer, but I see the hesitation in his eyes. He knows, deep down, that he's as much a prisoner of this place as I am. We all are, in one way or another. The only difference is, I'm aware of my chains. I've learned to live with them, to turn them into something I can control.

The session goes on like this—more questions, more games. By the time it's over, Dr. Hayes looks as drained as ever, his shoulders slumped under the weight of his own questions. He nods to the orderly outside, and the door clicks shut behind him as he leaves.

I sit there for a moment, staring at the door, the faint sound of his footsteps fading away. The room is quiet again, but the silence feels different now.

The whispers in the dark aren't gone. They never are.

They're just waiting for the next move.

Chapter 2: The Breaking Point

The room is colder today. Not physically colder, but in a way that seeps into the skin and lingers in the bones. The walls feel closer, the shadows darker, pressing in as if the very air is conspiring to suffocate me.

I hate the way this place feels at times, like it's shifting around me, watching me. I know it's all in my head, of course. But even knowing that doesn't make it stop.

They say I'm getting better—making "progress," as Dr. Hayes puts it. I don't correct him. It's easier to let them think what they want to think. Easier to play along with their expectations and give them the illusion that they're helping me. They're not, of course. But they need to believe they are.

I've always been good at giving people what they need.

The session with Dr. Hayes today is supposed to be a follow-up on what I said last time. Control. He was fascinated by that word, as if I'd unlocked some hidden truth for him. It's almost laughable, watching him scribble notes and nod thoughtfully, pretending to understand. But the truth is something he can't reach. Control is more than just a concept; it's everything. And right now, it's slipping through my fingers.

It started a few days ago, in the dead of night. I was lying in my bed, staring at the ceiling, counting the cracks like I always do when sleep refuses to come. But something was different this time. The room felt wrong. The air was thick with something I couldn't quite name, a tension that crawled under my skin and made me restless.

I sat up, my eyes scanning the darkness, searching for the source of that feeling. But there was nothing. Just the usual shadows, the dim outline of the door, the faint glow of the streetlight filtering through the tiny window. Everything was the same, and yet it wasn't.

That's when I heard it. A sound, faint at first, like a whisper brushing against the edge of my consciousness. I froze, straining to listen, but the sound was gone as quickly as it had come. My pulse quickened, my mind racing with questions, but I stayed still, my body tense and alert.

Minutes passed, maybe hours—I'm not sure. Time blurs in this place. But eventually, the whisper came again, this time louder, more distinct. A single word, spoken in a voice that wasn't mine.

"Run."

It was so clear, so sharp, that for a moment, I thought someone was in the room with me. I glanced around, my eyes scanning every corner, but the room was empty. Just me and the shadows.

I wanted to ignore it, to dismiss it as a trick of the mind, but the word echoed in my head, bouncing around like a trapped thought. Run. It made no sense. Where would I run to? There's nowhere to go, not in this place. The doors are locked, the hallways are guarded, and even if I did manage to escape, where would I go?

But the whisper wouldn't leave me alone. It kept coming back, night after night, growing louder each time. It wasn't just a word anymore—it was a command. And I could feel it gnawing at me, pulling me toward something I didn't understand.

I started losing sleep. My thoughts became jumbled, disjointed. I couldn't focus during the day, and the sessions with Dr. Hayes became harder to get through. I found myself drifting off in the middle of conversations, my mind slipping back to that whisper, to the voice that wasn't mine.

I told myself it didn't matter. That it was just a figment of my imagination, a side effect of being trapped in this place for too long. But deep down, I knew there was something more. Something I couldn't explain, something that was pulling me toward a breaking point.

That breaking point came today.

It started like any other session. Dr. Hayes, with his ever-present clipboard and tired smile, asked me the same old questions. How are you feeling? Have you been sleeping? Have you had any more thoughts about control?

I answered like I always do, with just enough truth to keep him satisfied, but not enough to give him any real insight. He nodded, jotting down notes, his pen scratching against the paper in a rhythm that made my skin crawl.

But then he asked something different.

"Have you been hearing anything unusual?"

The question caught me off guard. My mind immediately flashed to the whisper, but I didn't say anything. I couldn't. If I told him about it, he'd think I was losing it. And that would mean more tests, more questions, more time locked away in this room.

So I shook my head. "No," I said, my voice steady. "Nothing unusual."

He didn't believe me. I could see it in his eyes, the way they narrowed slightly, the way his pen hesitated over the paper. He knew I was hiding something, but he didn't push. Not yet.

Instead, he leaned back in his chair and crossed his legs, his eyes never leaving mine. "You know, Elise," he began, his voice calm and measured, "it's normal to experience certain... anomalies when you're going through a process like this. Your mind is adjusting, trying to make sense of everything. Sometimes, that means you'll hear things, or see things that aren't really there."

He paused, waiting for my reaction. I gave him nothing.

"I've spoken with other patients," he continued, "who've experienced similar things. Voices, whispers, shadows in the corners of their vision. It's all part of the process of healing. The mind plays tricks when it's trying to process trauma."

Trauma. That word again. They love to throw it around like it explains everything.

"Have you experienced anything like that?" he asked, his eyes boring into mine.

I wanted to lie. I wanted to tell him no, that everything was fine, that I was making progress just like he wanted. But the whisper was there, lurking in the back of my mind, louder now, more insistent. Run.

My hands clenched into fists in my lap, my nails digging into my palms. The room felt smaller, the air heavier, pressing down on me from all sides. I could feel my pulse quickening, the blood rushing in my ears. Dr. Hayes was still watching me, waiting, his pen poised over the paper, ready to capture whatever I said next.

I couldn't breathe. The walls were closing in, suffocating me. The whisper was louder now, almost a scream, and I couldn't shut it out. Run. Run. RUN.

Without thinking, I bolted.

I was on my feet before I even realized what I was doing, the chair clattering to the floor behind me. Dr. Hayes shouted something, but I didn't hear him. My heart was pounding in my chest, my vision tunneling as I sprinted toward the door.

I don't know what I was thinking. There was nowhere to go, no way out. But in that moment, all I could hear was the whisper, driving me forward, pushing me to run, to escape.

I barely made it two steps before the orderlies grabbed me. Their hands were rough, strong, dragging me back toward the chair, pinning me down as I thrashed and kicked. Dr. Hayes was standing now, his face pale, his eyes wide with shock. He didn't expect this. He didn't expect me to break.

But I had. And now there was no going back.

They held me down, their grips like iron, and I could feel the weight of their bodies pressing against me, holding me in place. The room spun around me, the walls blurring together as the whisper screamed in my ears, deafening, overwhelming. RUN. RUN. RUN.

I couldn't move. I couldn't think. All I could do was scream.

The world went black.

When I woke up, I was back in my room. My wrists were sore from where the restraints had been, and my head throbbed with a dull ache. The whisper was gone, replaced by a thick, suffocating silence that pressed against my skull like a vice.

I don't know how long I lay there, staring at the ceiling, my mind blank and empty. Time didn't exist in this place. There was only the constant hum of the fluorescent lights, the distant shuffle of feet in the hallway, and the weight of my own thoughts pressing down on me like a lead blanket.

Eventually, the door opened, and an orderly stepped inside. He didn't say anything, just left a tray of food on the small table by the bed and walked out, locking the door behind him.

I didn't touch the food. I wasn't hungry.

All I could think about was what had happened in Dr. Hayes's office. The look on his face when I snapped, the way the orderlies had dragged me down, the cold, sterile feeling of the restraints against my skin.

I had lost control.

That thought sent a shiver down my spine. I had prided myself on always being in control, on playing their game, on giving them just enough to keep them satisfied. But now, the game was over. The mask had cracked, and I had shown them something they weren't supposed to see.

I had shown them weakness.

And in this place, weakness is a dangerous thing.

I sat up slowly, my body aching, and glanced toward the window. The streetlights outside flickered, casting eerie shadows across the room. I could feel the walls pressing in again, tighter this time, as if they knew I had failed.

But I wasn't beaten yet.

The whisper may have driven me to this point, but it wouldn't break me. Not completely. I had lost control, yes, but I could get it back. I had to.

Because in this place, control is the only thing that matters.

Chapter 3: Silent Games

There's a certain satisfaction that comes with being the smartest person in the room.

The way people hang on your every word, waiting, hoping to catch a glimpse of what's really going on in your mind—it's almost intoxicating. Watching their eyes flicker with uncertainty, their hands fidget nervously as they try to piece together what they think they know about you. But they never really know, do they?

The best part of the game is that they think they're the ones in control.

I sit across from Dr. Fredrickson now, her thin lips pursed into a faint smile that doesn't reach her eyes. She's new. New to the institution, new to me, new to all of this. The fresh ones are always the easiest to play. They come in with their optimism, thinking they'll be the ones to crack the case, to find the hidden key inside my mind and unlock whatever secrets lie buried there.

But I don't keep secrets. Not really. I just keep the truth hidden behind enough layers that no one bothers to dig deep enough to find it.

Dr. Fredrickson crosses her legs and leans forward slightly, clipboard in hand, her pen poised above the paper, ready to capture whatever groundbreaking insight she thinks I'm about to offer. She doesn't know yet that this is all part of the game.

"Let's start with something simple," she says, her voice calm, measured. "How are you feeling today?"

There it is. The first move.

I tilt my head slightly, letting my eyes drift lazily to the window behind her. The sky outside is a dull gray, the kind of color that makes you feel like you're trapped in some kind of eternal twilight. It fits, really. That's what this place is—an in-between. Not quite life, not quite death. Just... existing. A holding pattern.

"I'm fine," I say, my voice smooth, detached.

Dr. Fredrickson doesn't react. She's been trained for this. She knows not to let any sign of frustration or impatience show. But I can see the way her fingers tighten just a little around the pen, the way her eyes flicker ever so slightly when she realizes she's not going to get what she wants from me right away.

That's move two.

"Let's talk about your progress," she continues, adjusting her glasses on the bridge of her nose. "I've read your file. Dr. Hayes mentioned that you've been cooperative in your sessions with him. Is that true?"

I smile, just enough to keep her guessing. "I cooperate when it's necessary."

Her pen scratches against the paper, jotting down notes. I wonder what she's writing. "Patient displays selective cooperation," maybe. Or "resistant to opening up." It doesn't matter. Whatever she writes, it'll be wrong. Because she's already playing into my hands, whether she knows it or not.

"Why do you say 'when it's necessary'?" she asks, her tone soft, as if she's trying to coax me into revealing something deeper.

This is where the game gets interesting.

I lean back in my chair, crossing my arms over my chest, and meet her gaze. "I'm not here to waste my time. Or yours. If I'm going to talk, it's because I have something worth saying."

Dr. Fredrickson's eyes narrow, just for a moment, and I know I've hit a nerve. She wasn't expecting that. The new ones never are. They come in with their playbook of tactics, thinking they can guide me through some carefully crafted script. But they don't understand that I'm the one who writes the script.

She clears her throat, glancing down at her notes before speaking again. "You mentioned control in one of your earlier sessions. Can you tell me more about that? What does control mean to you?"

Control. That word again. It's funny how much they fixate on it. As if understanding what it means to me will somehow unlock the door to everything else.

I think for a moment, letting the silence hang between us like a thin thread. This is another part of the game—letting the silence build, making them uncomfortable with it. Most people can't stand silence. They feel the need to fill it, to say something, anything, just to break the tension. But I don't mind it. Silence is powerful. It gives me the upper hand.

Finally, I speak. "Control is... freedom. It's the only real freedom any of us have."

Dr. Fredrickson nods slowly, her pen moving across the paper again. "And do you feel like you have control here, in this place?"

I laugh. It's a soft, quiet sound, but it cuts through the room like a knife. "Control? In here? No. They make sure you don't have control over anything in this place. Not your schedule, not your food, not your body. Hell, I'm not even allowed to close my own door."

The pen pauses, just for a second. I see her scribble something, maybe a shift in her perception of me. Then, she leans forward again, her voice quieter now, more intimate. "But there are things you can control, aren't there? Your thoughts, your actions, how you choose to respond to what's happening around you."

I shrug, looking away again. "Thoughts aren't always something you can control."

I see her reaction in the corner of my eye—a slight tightening of her jaw, her fingers flexing around the pen. She thinks she's hit something important. She thinks she's getting closer.

I'm tempted to let her believe that for a little while.

"I want to understand," she says softly. "I want to help you, Elise."

Elise. The name they gave me. The name that doesn't belong to me.

I turn my head slowly, meeting her gaze with cold, unwavering eyes. "You can't help me."

Dr. Fredrickson doesn't flinch, but I see the way her body shifts, just slightly. She's uncomfortable, and I can feel the balance of power tipping back in my favor.

This is move three.

"I don't believe that," she says. "Everyone can be helped. You just have to be willing to let someone in."

I almost laugh at that. It's such a cliché, such a predictable line from someone who thinks they understand how the mind works. But that's the thing about people like her—they think they can fix everything with enough time, enough patience. They don't understand that some things aren't broken. Some things are exactly the way they're supposed to be.

She wants me to let her in. But she doesn't realize that the door she's trying to open leads nowhere.

The game continues like this for the rest of the session. Dr. Fredrickson asks her carefully crafted questions, and I give her just enough to keep her on the hook, but never enough to let her really see anything. I control the narrative, guiding her down whatever path I choose, knowing that she'll follow wherever I lead.

By the end, she's left with more questions than answers, and I'm left with the quiet satisfaction of knowing that I'm still in control.

As she gathers her notes and prepares to leave, she gives me one last look. It's the look of someone who thinks they've only scratched the surface, who believes that there's still more to uncover. I can see the determination in her eyes, the belief that if she just tries hard enough, she'll be the one to crack the code.

But she won't.

No one ever does.

After Dr. Fredrickson leaves, the room feels emptier. Colder. The silence stretches out, filling the space she's left behind, and I can feel the familiar weight of the walls pressing in again. This place, this sterile, colorless cage, it's designed to make you feel small. Powerless.

But I'm not powerless. Not yet.

I walk to the window and press my hand against the cold glass. Outside, the sky is still that same dull gray, the world beyond the institution moving on without me. I wonder if anyone out there knows I exist. If they care. Probably not. People like me aren't the kind they think about. We're hidden away, locked up, kept out of sight so the world can pretend we don't exist.

But I exist.

And I'm not going to stay here forever.

A knock at the door pulls me from my thoughts. I turn just as the orderly steps inside, his expression blank, professional. He doesn't say anything as he sets down my dinner tray on the small table in the corner. I don't bother looking at the food. It's always the same—bland, tasteless, barely enough to keep me going.

The orderly glances at me, his eyes lingering for just a second longer than usual. I wonder what he's thinking. Does he see me the way the doctors do? As some kind of puzzle to be solved? Or does he see me as something else—something dangerous?

He leaves without a word, and the door clicks shut behind him.

I sit down on the bed, staring at the tray of food, but not really seeing it. My mind is elsewhere, replaying the session with Dr. Fredrickson, analyzing every move, every word, every gesture. She's going to be a challenge. She's not like the others. She's sharper, more observant. She's not going to fall for the same tricks.

I'll have to be more careful with her.

The thought doesn't bother me. If anything, it excites me. A new challenge, a new game to play. And I always win.

The next few days pass in a blur. My sessions with Dr. Fredrickson continue, each one more intense than the last. She pushes harder, asks more probing questions, but I remain in control, steering the conversation where I want it to go.

But there's something else. Something I didn't expect.

Dr. Hayes.

He visits me again, unannounced, slipping into the room like a shadow. His presence is different now—more focused, more intense. He doesn't waste time with pleasantries or small talk. Instead, he sits down across from me, his eyes locking onto mine, and asks a single question.

"Are you afraid, Elise?"

The question catches me off guard. It's not part of the game. It's not what I was expecting.

For the first time in a long time, I don't have an immediate answer.

He leans forward, his gaze never wavering. "I've been watching you. Listening to what you say. And I can't help but wonder if, underneath it all, you're afraid. Not of me. Not of this place. But of yourself."

The air feels heavier, thicker, like the room itself is holding its breath.

"You think you're in control," Dr. Hayes continues, his voice calm, steady. "But what if you're not? What if the control you think you have is just another illusion?"

I don't respond. I can't.

Because deep down, in the part of my mind that I've tried to ignore, I know he's right.

Control is a fragile thing. And once it starts to slip, there's no getting it back.

Chapter 4: Breaking Points

The air was thick with unspoken words as I sat on the edge of my bed, the sterile white walls closing in like a vise. The dull, flickering overhead light cast harsh shadows, creating an unsettling contrast against the backdrop of my mind—a landscape filled with chaos and control. I could hear the faint hum of the fluorescent bulbs overhead, a constant reminder of the world outside, a world I was locked away from.

Days had passed since Dr. Hayes's unexpected visit, and the implications of his words haunted me like a specter. *What if you're not in control?* The question replayed in my mind like a broken record, each repetition digging deeper into the recesses of my thoughts. I had built my entire existence around the illusion of control, crafting a fortress within my mind to keep the chaos at bay. But what if that fortress was crumbling?

A sharp knock on the door broke my reverie, jolting me back to reality. I turned my head, my heartbeat quickening. The orderly stepped in, his expression as blank as ever. He set down my breakfast tray with a clatter that echoed in the silence. I didn't bother to look at the food. I never did. Instead, I focused on the orderly's eyes, searching for any hint of understanding or recognition. Did he see the real me? Or was I just another case file in a long line of forgotten names?

"Your session with Dr. Fredrickson is in fifteen minutes," he said, his tone monotone. He glanced at me, and for a brief moment, I caught a flicker of something—curiosity, perhaps?—before it was smothered by professionalism.

"Thank you," I replied, my voice steady despite the storm brewing inside. He nodded and left the room, the door clicking shut with a finality that sent a shiver down my spine.

I rose from the bed, pacing the small space. My thoughts churned, a whirlpool of uncertainty and defiance. Dr. Fredrickson had been relentless in her pursuit of truth, her probing questions a relentless tide against my carefully constructed walls. But today, I would not yield. Today, I would remind her who was truly in control.

As I entered the small therapy room, I took a moment to absorb the environment—the sterile white walls adorned with abstract art that felt more suffocating than inspiring, the minimalist furniture that offered no comfort. Dr. Fredrickson was already seated, her clipboard balanced on her knee, her pen poised above the page. Her expression was unreadable, a mask of professionalism that belied the tension in the air.

"Good morning, Elise," she said, her voice calm and measured. "How are you feeling today?"

I took my seat across from her, a sly smile playing on my lips. "I'm fine," I replied, echoing my previous answer. It was a phrase I had mastered, a simple shield to deflect any probing attempts.

She studied me for a moment, her eyes narrowing slightly as if trying to decipher a code. "Fine can mean many things. Are you feeling fine emotionally? Mentally?"

I shrugged, leaning back in my chair. "I'm not here to analyze my feelings, Doctor. I'm here to have a conversation."

Dr. Fredrickson's expression didn't waver, but I could sense the shift in her demeanor. "Then let's talk. I've noticed you often mention control in our sessions. Can you elaborate on why it's such an important concept for you?"

The question was expected, yet I relished the opportunity to steer the conversation. "Control is the foundation of existence. Without it, we're at the mercy of external forces. I refuse to let that happen."

Her pen scratched against the paper, documenting my words as if they held the key to my psyche. "And how do you maintain that control in this environment? Do you feel it slipping away?"

The challenge in her voice ignited a spark of defiance within me. "I maintain control by not allowing anyone to see the real me. As long as I can keep you guessing, I'm the one pulling the strings."

She leaned forward, her eyes glinting with interest. "But isn't that a fragile game? If you're always in disguise, how can you ever truly connect with anyone?"

I let out a low chuckle, relishing the moment. "Connection is overrated. People are just as likely to betray you as they are to support you. Trust is a risk I'm not willing to take."

Dr. Fredrickson's expression softened, her pen hovering over the page. "And yet, you're here. You're engaging with me. Doesn't that imply some level of trust?"

The question hung in the air like a challenge. I paused, contemplating my response. "I engage because I choose to. Because it amuses me to play this game. But trust? That's a different matter entirely."

The silence stretched between us, thickening with tension. I could see the wheels turning in her mind, the way she was searching for an angle, a weakness to exploit. But I was too far ahead of her. I was the architect of this game, and I would dictate the rules.

"Let's talk about your relationship with Dr. Hayes," she said, shifting tactics. "You seem to react differently to him than to me."

I tilted my head, intrigued. "Different how?"

"You seem more guarded with me, but with him, there's a flicker of something else. Curiosity, perhaps? A willingness to engage beyond the surface?"

"Or maybe I just find him amusing," I countered, a smirk forming on my lips. "He's like a dog chasing its tail, always circling back to the same questions."

Dr. Fredrickson's eyes narrowed again, a flash of frustration crossing her features. "You're avoiding the question, Elise. Are you afraid of what he might uncover?"

I leaned back further, folding my arms across my chest. "Fear is a weakness I refuse to acknowledge. Besides, I'm not the one being examined here."

She jotted down notes, her brow furrowed in concentration. "But you're aware that the more you resist, the more curiosity you provoke. It's a double-edged sword."

The irony of her words didn't escape me. I was a master of provocation, always pushing boundaries to see how far I could go. "Curiosity is a human flaw. People are drawn to what they don't understand, and I'm more than a puzzle to be solved."

"Then let's explore that. What do you believe is driving your need for control? Is it a reaction to trauma? A way to cope with your circumstances?"

I feigned contemplation, a playful glimmer in my eye. "Perhaps I just enjoy the thrill of it all. The chase, the manipulation. Why would I want to let anyone in when it's so much more entertaining to keep them guessing?"

Dr. Fredrickson's expression remained steadfast, but I could see her resolve wavering. "But at what cost, Elise? You're isolating yourself, shutting out potential connections that could aid in your healing."

I scoffed, dismissing her concern. "Healing? This place is a farce. You think you can fix me with your little sessions and your probing questions? I'm not broken; I'm just... different."

"Different can be beautiful," she replied softly. "But it can also be a prison if you don't allow anyone in."

I leaned forward, narrowing my eyes. "You want to help? Then stop trying to analyze me. I'm not a case study. I'm a person, and I won't be reduced to your clinical terms."

Her gaze softened, and for a moment, I saw a flicker of understanding. But just as quickly, it was gone, replaced by the practiced façade of a therapist. "Elise, this is about more than just words. It's about understanding the motivations behind them. What are you afraid of? What are you hiding?"

The question hit me like a punch to the gut, a moment of vulnerability that I couldn't allow. I pushed back, fortifying my defenses. "I'm not hiding anything. I'm simply choosing not to share."

"Choosing not to share implies a reason," she pressed. "What's so terrible that you can't speak it?"

I felt the walls around me start to tremble, a crack in the facade I had built so carefully. "You think I owe you an explanation? I don't. My past is mine, and it doesn't concern you."

"Perhaps, but understanding your past could illuminate the path forward," she replied gently. "Every person carries their burdens. It's part of being human."

I bristled at her words, feeling the heat rise in my cheeks. "Humanity is overrated. People are selfish, driven by their desires and their fears. They will turn on you in an instant."

"And yet, you're here, engaging with me. That indicates a desire for something more," she countered, her voice calm and steady. "You might be afraid, but you're also seeking connection, even if it's in the smallest way."

The accusation stung, and I struggled to maintain my composure. "Connection is a double-edged sword. It opens you up to pain and betrayal. Why would I willingly step into that?"

"Because it's through connection that we find understanding and healing," she said softly, her gaze steady. "You're isolating yourself, and that's a dangerous path."

The sincerity in her voice momentarily shook my resolve, but I quickly buried it. "I'm not afraid of isolation. It's comfortable. I know how to navigate it."

"Do you? Or is it just another way to mask the pain?" she pressed, her tone gentle yet firm.

I opened my mouth to respond, but the words caught in my throat. The truth of her statement echoed in my mind, sending ripples of doubt through my carefully constructed walls. The silence stretched between us, heavy and charged.

"Maybe it's time to confront those feelings, Elise," she continued, her voice softer now. "What are you afraid of losing if you let someone in?"

I wanted to scream, to lash out at her for pushing me, for daring to question my defenses. But instead, I sat in silence, grappling with the tumult inside me. What was I afraid of? The answer flickered just out of reach, elusive and painful.

"Let's take a moment," Dr. Fredrickson suggested, her voice a soothing balm amidst the chaos. "Breathe. Focus on the present. What do you feel in this moment?"

I closed my eyes, the familiar weight of the world pressing down on me. The sterile smell of the room, the distant sounds of life outside, the beating of my own heart. But beneath it all lay an undercurrent of fear, a whisper of vulnerability that threatened to unravel everything I had built.

"I feel... trapped," I admitted, my voice barely above a whisper. "Trapped in this place, in my mind, in my past."

Dr. Fredrickson's gaze softened, a glimmer of understanding shining through. "And that feeling of being trapped—what does it bring up for you? Is it the fear of losing control?"

"Yes," I breathed, the admission feeling like a weight lifting. "Control is all I have. Without it, I'm nothing."

"Control can feel like safety, but it can also be a cage," she replied gently. "What would it take for you to feel safe enough to let go, even just a little?"

The question hung in the air, challenging me to confront the heart of my fears. I hesitated, the silence stretching uncomfortably as I grappled with the vulnerability of the moment. What would it take? The answer felt terrifyingly simple.

"Trust," I finally whispered, the word escaping my lips like a confession. "Trust in someone else... trust that they won't hurt me."

Dr. Fredrickson nodded, a small smile breaking through her professional demeanor. "And that's a brave admission, Elise. Trust isn't easy, especially when you've been hurt before. But it's a risk worth taking."

The walls I had built began to tremble, and I felt the first cracks of doubt seep through. Could I let someone in? Could I risk everything I had built to embrace vulnerability?

"Do you trust me?" she asked, her tone gentle yet firm.

I took a deep breath, the weight of the question pressing down on me. "I don't know."

"Then let's work on that," she said softly. "Let's explore the reasons behind that distrust and see if we can find a way forward together."

The challenge hung in the air, an invitation to step beyond the boundaries I had so carefully crafted. Could I take that step? Could I allow myself to be vulnerable, even for a moment?

I felt a flicker of something deep within—a spark of hope mixed with trepidation. "Maybe... maybe I can try."

"Trying is all we can do," she replied, her voice a soothing balm against my fears. "Let's take it one step at a time."

The tension in the room shifted, and for the first time, I felt a glimmer of connection amidst the chaos. Maybe I could let someone in, just a little. Maybe there was a path forward that didn't require me to bear the weight of my past alone.

As the session continued, the conversation flowed more freely. I found myself sharing snippets of my life, the fragments I had kept buried beneath layers of denial. Each revelation felt like a small victory, a step toward breaking down the walls I had built.

The more I spoke, the more I realized that vulnerability didn't equate to weakness. It was a form of strength, a willingness to confront the truths I had been hiding from for so long. And in that moment of realization, I felt a shift within me.

"Let's talk about the things you're afraid to face," Dr. Fredrickson encouraged, her tone gentle yet firm. "What are the shadows lurking in your past?"

The question sent a jolt through me, and I hesitated, grappling with the memories that threatened to surface. But as I met her gaze, I saw a flicker of understanding, a reminder that I was not alone in this journey.

With a deep breath, I began to unravel the threads of my past, each revelation bringing me closer to the light I had been so desperately avoiding. I spoke of my childhood, of the fractures that had shaped me, the betrayals that had left scars. I spoke of moments of joy and heartache, of the people who had come and gone, leaving imprints on my soul.

As the words poured from me, I felt a sense of liberation, as if I was shedding layers of armor that had weighed me down for so long. The shadows that had once consumed me began to fade, replaced by a growing sense of clarity.

In that moment, I understood that healing was not a destination but a journey—a winding path filled with twists and turns, a tapestry woven from threads of pain and resilience. And as I embraced that journey, I felt the weight of my past lift, replaced by a flicker of hope.

Dr. Fredrickson listened intently, her expression unwavering as I shared my truth. There was no judgment in her gaze, only empathy and understanding. With each revelation, I felt the walls of my fortress begin to crumble, replaced by a fragile but blossoming sense of connection.

As the session drew to a close, I realized that I had taken a step toward something I had long avoided—a willingness to confront my fears and embrace vulnerability. The journey ahead would not be easy, but for the first time, I felt a flicker of hope—a belief that maybe, just maybe, I could learn to trust again.

"I don't know what the future holds," I admitted as I stood to leave, a sense of uncertainty swirling within me. "But I'm willing to try."

Dr. Fredrickson smiled, her eyes shining with encouragement. "That's all we can do, Elise. One step at a time."

As I left the therapy room, I felt a weight lift from my shoulders, the echoes of my past fading into the distance. The road ahead would be challenging, but I was no longer alone. I had taken the first step toward healing, and with it came a sense of freedom—a freedom to be imperfect, to embrace my flaws, and to let someone in.

In that moment, as I walked down the sterile hallway of the institution, I felt the walls closing in less. I was ready to face whatever lay ahead, armed with the knowledge that I had the power to redefine my narrative. And as I took a deep breath, I felt the flicker of hope grow stronger—a beacon guiding me toward the light beyond the shadows.

Chapter 5: Shattered Illusions

The world outside my window felt like a distant dream—a blurry landscape of sunlight and shadows that danced just out of reach. Each day blended into the next, the monotony of my existence a cruel reminder of the freedom I had once taken for granted. But today was different. Today, I felt a flicker of hope igniting within me, a small ember that threatened to grow into a flame.

The therapy session with Dr. Fredrickson had shaken me in ways I hadn't anticipated. For the first time, I had dared to peel back the layers of my carefully constructed façade, exposing the raw, vulnerable parts of myself that I had hidden for so long. And while the fear of judgment still loomed in the back of my mind, I was beginning to realize that perhaps vulnerability didn't equate to weakness. Maybe it was the key to healing.

As I sat on the edge of my bed, I ran my fingers over the fabric of the worn quilt, tracing the intricate patterns that had faded over time. Each stitch held a memory—a fragment of my past that had woven itself into the fabric of my identity. I closed my eyes, allowing the memories to wash over me, a tidal wave of emotions threatening to drown me. But I stood firm, determined to face them head-on.

The sound of the door creaking open broke my reverie, and I looked up to see Dr. Hayes entering the room. His presence filled the space, an aura of calm mixed with curiosity. I felt a surge of defiance rise within me, but I quickly suppressed it. This wasn't the time for games.

"Good morning, Elise," he greeted, his voice warm and inviting. "How are you feeling today?"

I hesitated, searching for the right words. "I'm... getting there. I suppose."

"Getting there is a step in the right direction," he said with a nod, his expression encouraging. "Can we talk about what's been on your mind since our last session?"

I shifted in my seat, feeling the weight of his gaze upon me. I had never been one to open up easily, but something about Dr. Hayes made it feel less like an interrogation and more like a conversation between equals. "I've been thinking a lot about control and what it means to truly let go," I admitted, my voice steady despite the turmoil within.

"Letting go can be a powerful act," he replied, his tone thoughtful. "It requires a level of trust, both in yourself and in others. What do you think has been holding you back from that trust?"

I clenched my fists, the familiar walls of defensiveness rising up to shield me from his probing questions. "Fear," I confessed, the word slipping out before I could stop it. "Fear of getting hurt, fear of losing everything I've worked so hard to build."

"Fear is a natural response," he said gently. "But it can also be a cage, keeping you trapped in a cycle of isolation. What if you allowed yourself to step outside of that cage, even just for a moment?"

I paused, the weight of his words settling over me like a heavy blanket. Stepping outside my cage felt terrifying, like standing on the edge of a precipice with no safety net below. "What if I fall?" I whispered, the vulnerability of the question hanging in the air.

"Then you learn to fly," he replied, his smile warm and genuine. "And if you do fall, you have people here who will help you get back up. You don't have to do this alone."

The sincerity in his words sent a shiver down my spine, stirring something deep within me. I had spent so long in isolation, believing that I was the only one who could navigate the chaos of my mind. But what if I didn't have to bear that burden alone?

"Maybe I'm just not ready," I admitted, the honesty of my admission surprising even me. "Maybe I need more time."

"Time is a valuable commodity," Dr. Hayes said, leaning forward slightly. "But remember that growth often happens outside of our comfort zones. It's okay to take your time, but don't let it become an excuse to stay stagnant."

His words resonated with me, echoing the sentiment Dr. Fredrickson had shared during our session. The idea of growth, of pushing past my boundaries, began to take root in my mind. But as the seeds of hope began to sprout, the shadows of doubt loomed larger than ever.

"I want to believe that," I said slowly, the conflict within me bubbling to the surface. "But every time I take a step forward, I feel like I'm two steps back. It's exhausting."

Dr. Hayes nodded, his expression thoughtful. "Progress isn't always linear. It's messy and unpredictable, and that's okay. What matters is that you keep moving forward, even if it feels small. Every step counts."

I couldn't help but admire his unwavering positivity, a stark contrast to the storm swirling inside me. I felt as if I were standing on the precipice of something monumental, teetering between the desire for change and the fear of what that change might bring.

"What if I fail?" I asked, my voice barely above a whisper. "What if I try to let go, only to find out I'm not strong enough?"

"Failure is a part of life, Elise," he replied, his tone gentle yet firm. "It's how we learn and grow. But the fear of failure shouldn't keep you from trying. Remember, every great achievement comes with its share of failures."

His words hung in the air, a lifeline thrown into the turbulent sea of my emotions. "I suppose you're right," I conceded reluctantly. "But I don't know how to begin."

"Start small," he suggested. "What's one thing you could do today that would challenge your perception of control? It could be as simple as engaging in a conversation with someone or allowing yourself to be vulnerable in a small way."

The idea of vulnerability sent a shiver of fear coursing through me, but beneath it lay a flicker of excitement. "Maybe I could try talking to one of the other patients," I said slowly, the idea forming as I spoke. "I've been avoiding them, but perhaps I should reach out."

"That sounds like a great step," Dr. Hayes encouraged. "Connecting with others can help you realize you're not alone in this. You might find comfort in shared experiences."

I considered his words, a mixture of trepidation and curiosity swirling within me. Could I really take that step? The thought of opening up to someone else felt daunting, but a part of me craved connection—the warmth of companionship amidst the coldness of isolation.

"Okay," I said finally, my resolve strengthening. "I'll give it a try."

Dr. Hayes smiled, his eyes shining with encouragement. "That's the spirit. Just remember to be kind to yourself along the way. Growth takes time, and it's okay to stumble."

As our session came to a close, I felt a renewed sense of purpose stirring within me. I had spent far too long clinging to my fears, and it was time to embrace the uncertainty of change. I stood up, a sense of determination flooding my veins.

"Thank you," I said, my voice steady. "I appreciate your guidance."

"Anytime, Elise," he replied, his smile genuine. "I believe in you."

As I stepped out of the therapy room, a surge of adrenaline coursed through me. I was ready to face the unknown, to take that first tentative step into the world beyond my fortress of solitude. The thought of engaging with the other patients both excited and terrified me, but I was willing to embrace that discomfort.

I wandered through the dimly lit corridors of the institution, each step echoing against the sterile walls. The air felt charged with possibility, and I could feel the weight of my past lifting ever so slightly.

My heart raced as I approached the common area, where a small group of patients sat together, their laughter mingling with the soft murmur of conversation.

Taking a deep breath, I gathered my courage and approached them. They glanced up as I approached, their expressions a mix of curiosity and warmth. "Mind if I join you?" I asked, forcing a smile despite the flutter of anxiety in my stomach.

"Of course!" one of them replied, a friendly grin lighting up her face. "We were just discussing our favorite books. What about you?"

Relief washed over me as I settled into the circle, the tension in my shoulders easing. "I love reading," I said, my voice growing more confident as I spoke. "Lately, I've been getting into psychological thrillers. They're fascinating."

The group leaned in, their interest piqued. "Oh, have you read 'The Silent Patient'?" another patient asked, his eyes bright with excitement.

"Yes! I loved that one," I replied, feeling a genuine connection start to form. "The twists in the story were incredible."

As we continued to talk, I felt a warmth spreading through me—a sense of belonging that I hadn't felt in a long time. I shared my thoughts and opinions, and they listened intently, responding with laughter and shared experiences. The conversation flowed effortlessly, each moment chipping away at the walls I had built around my heart.

For the first time in what felt like an eternity, I realized that I wasn't alone in this battle. Each person in the group carried their own burdens, their own stories of struggle and resilience. And together, we formed a tapestry of shared experiences—a reminder that even in our darkest moments, we could find light in one another.

As the hours passed, I found myself losing track of time, the laughter and camaraderie weaving a new sense of reality. It was liberating, exhilarating even, to let go of my carefully constructed defenses, if only for a moment. I discovered that connection could be a balm for the soul, a salve for the wounds that had festered for far too long.

Eventually, the sun began to dip below the horizon, casting a warm golden glow over the room. I glanced around at the faces of my newfound companions, a sense of gratitude swelling within me. "Thank you for including me," I said, my voice filled with sincerity. "I really enjoyed this."

"Anytime," one of them replied, a twinkle of mischief in her eyes. "You're one of us now!"

As I made my way back to my room, the exhilaration of the evening coursed through my veins. I felt lighter, unburdened by the weight of my fears. The shadows that had once loomed over me began to recede, replaced by the flicker of hope that had ignited during my session with Dr. Hayes.

But as I settled into bed, exhaustion creeping in, I couldn't shake the lingering doubts that danced at the edges of my mind. What if this newfound connection was fleeting? What if I stumbled and fell, unable to rise again? The fear gnawed at me, a reminder of the darkness that still lurked beneath the surface.

But as I closed my eyes, I felt a flicker of defiance rising within me—a determination to push through the shadows and embrace the light. I had taken a step forward, and with it came a newfound sense of strength. I wouldn't allow fear to dictate my path any longer.

In the stillness of the night, I whispered a silent promise to myself: to embrace vulnerability, to seek connection, and to face the unknown with courage. The journey ahead would be filled with challenges, but I was no longer alone. I had taken the first step toward healing, and for the first time, I felt ready to chase the normal I had longed for.

As sleep began to pull me under, I felt the warmth of hope enveloping me—a comforting embrace that whispered of possibilities yet to come. And as I drifted off into the realm of dreams, I knew that tomorrow would bring new opportunities for growth, for connection, and for the chance to redefine my story.

Chapter 6: Fragments Of Truth

The morning light filtered through the thin curtains of my room, casting soft patterns on the walls. As I sat up, I felt a strange mixture of anticipation and apprehension swirling within me. Yesterday had been a breakthrough, a moment when I had dared to connect with others. Yet today loomed like a blank canvas, both inviting and intimidating. What would I do with the newfound courage I had discovered?

After a quick shower, I dressed in comfortable clothes, the fabric a gentle embrace against my skin. I glanced in the mirror, taking a moment to assess the reflection staring back at me. The shadows beneath my eyes hinted at the sleepless nights I had endured, but today, there was something different—a flicker of determination in my gaze. Today would be about taking more steps toward my own healing, but I still felt the remnants of fear tugging at my thoughts.

I decided to venture into the common area early, hoping to find the other patients before the day's scheduled activities began. As I made my way through the corridors, I could hear snippets of laughter and conversation drifting from different rooms. The walls, once oppressive and cold, now felt alive with energy, a reminder that I wasn't alone in this journey.

When I arrived, I found the group gathered in a circle, playing a board game. The atmosphere was lighthearted, filled with laughter and friendly banter. I felt a warm rush of excitement as I approached. "Mind if I join?" I asked, my voice steady, yet tinged with nervousness.

"Of course!" the same girl from yesterday, Sarah, beamed at me. "We could use another player! It's all about teamwork and strategy!"

As I settled in beside her, I felt a wave of comfort wash over me. The familiarity of laughter and competition created a sense of belonging that soothed the edges of my anxiety. I took a deep breath, allowing the energy of the group to wash over me as we engaged in spirited discussions about strategies and personal anecdotes.

The game unfolded, filled with unexpected twists and turns that kept us all on our toes. I found myself laughing freely, the worries that had clung to me fading into the background. Each roll of the dice felt like a step toward embracing the uncertainties of life. For the first time in a long while, I felt the heavy weight of isolation begin to lift, replaced by the buoyancy of camaraderie.

As the game progressed, the conversations drifted into more personal territories. "So, what brought you here?" one of the other players asked me, his tone curious yet respectful. The question hung in the air, and I felt a familiar wave of apprehension wash over me. It was one thing to share laughter, but sharing my story felt like venturing into treacherous waters.

"Um, it's a bit complicated," I said, my voice faltering slightly. "I've been struggling with... well, a lot of things. Anxiety, mostly."

"Same here," Sarah chimed in, her expression sympathetic. "It can be really isolating, can't it?"

I nodded, the understanding in her gaze anchoring me. "It really can. I used to think I was alone in my struggles, like no one else could possibly understand."

"Honestly, that's why I love this place," another patient, Tom, added. "We're all in this together. It's nice to be able to share without judgment."

The words struck a chord within me, and I felt a sense of relief wash over me. In that moment, the barriers I had built around myself began to crumble. I realized that sharing my story didn't mean exposing my weaknesses; it meant opening a door to connection and empathy.

"I've spent a lot of time feeling like I had to face everything on my own," I admitted, feeling the warmth of vulnerability settle over me. "But it's comforting to know that I'm not the only one."

The group nodded in understanding, each of us sharing glances that spoke volumes. There was something powerful about being in the presence of others who had also weathered their own storms. In this shared space, we were not defined by our struggles, but rather by our resilience and willingness to confront the darkness.

As the game concluded, we transitioned into casual conversation, the atmosphere charged with camaraderie. We shared our favorite movies, books, and even our guilty pleasures, the laughter ringing out like a balm for our souls. I found myself fully present in these moments, the anxieties that usually clouded my mind momentarily forgotten.

But as the sun began to set, casting long shadows across the room, I felt a familiar unease creeping back in. The evening's lightness stood in stark contrast to the heaviness that sometimes enveloped me. Despite the laughter, I was acutely aware that the darkness still lurked beneath the surface, waiting for the opportune moment to strike.

Later that night, as I lay in bed, I couldn't shake the feeling of dread settling in my chest. The connections I had forged throughout the day felt fragile, like a delicate glass sculpture that could shatter at any moment. What if I let them in, only to find that I was unworthy of their friendship? The doubts clawed at me, threatening to unravel the progress I had made.

Determined to push through, I grabbed my journal from the bedside table. The pages held my thoughts, fears, and dreams—a cathartic release that had become my lifeline. As I penned my feelings, I reflected on the day's events, focusing on the moments that had sparked joy within me. But as I wrote, the shadows of self-doubt reemerged, threatening to suffocate the light I had found.

I had started this journey with the belief that healing was a linear path, a progression from darkness into light. But now, I realized that healing was anything but straightforward. It was a winding road filled with bumps, detours, and occasional plunges into darkness. Each step forward felt precarious, yet I was determined to embrace the process, no matter how messy it became.

In the days that followed, I continued to engage with the other patients, each interaction deepening the sense of connection that had begun to blossom. But just as I felt I was making strides, life had a way of throwing curveballs.

One afternoon, as we gathered for a group therapy session, I noticed a tension hanging in the air. The usual jovial atmosphere was replaced with an undercurrent of apprehension. Dr. Hayes entered the room, his expression grave.

"Thank you all for coming," he began, his voice steady but tinged with concern. "I want to address something that's been weighing on all of us. One of our fellow patients, Mia, has decided to leave the program."

A hush fell over the room as we processed the news. Mia had been a quiet presence in our group, a gentle soul with a kind smile. Her departure felt like a void, a gap that could not easily be filled. The weight of her absence settled heavily upon us.

"She felt that she needed to take a different path for her healing," Dr. Hayes continued, his gaze sweeping across the group. "It's important to remember that everyone's journey is unique. While we may feel a sense of loss, we must honor her decision."

As he spoke, I felt a knot forming in my stomach. The fragility of our connections was laid bare before me, and the fear of abandonment washed over me like a tidal wave. If Mia could leave, what did that mean for the rest of us? Would we, too, find ourselves grappling with the uncertainty of connection and disconnection?

The discussion shifted as we shared our thoughts about Mia's departure, each person expressing their feelings of loss and concern. As the conversation unfolded, I felt my own fears bubbling to the surface, a mixture of anger and sadness coiling tightly in my chest.

"Why didn't she talk to any of us?" I found myself asking, my voice trembling slightly. "Did she feel like she didn't belong?"

"No one truly knows what's going on in someone else's mind," Sarah responded gently. "We're all struggling in our own ways, and sometimes, that can make it hard to reach out."

"But we could have been there for her," I pressed, the frustration spilling out. "I just wish she had given us a chance."

"Sometimes it's difficult for people to see the support that's available to them," Dr. Hayes interjected. "We can't control the choices others make, no matter how much we may want to. The best we can do is to keep showing up for one another."

His words settled over the room, a somber reminder of the reality we faced. Each of us was on our individual journeys, navigating the complexities of our emotions and healing. But the fear of loss lingered, a shadow that would not easily dissipate.

As the session came to a close, I felt a heavy weight in my chest. I had opened myself up to connection, only to face the potential for heartbreak. The fragility of our relationships felt overwhelming, and I couldn't shake the thought that perhaps I was destined to lose everyone I allowed myself to care for.

That night, I found myself restless, tossing and turning as the shadows of doubt crept back into my mind. The feeling of isolation pressed in on me, suffocating and oppressive. I felt as if I was teetering on the edge of a precipice, the abyss below beckoning me to take a leap into the unknown.

In a moment of desperation, I grabbed my journal again, pouring my thoughts onto the pages. "Why do I keep allowing myself to feel this way? Why do I keep seeking connection only to be faced with the reality of loss?" I wrote furiously, the words flowing from my heart like a torrent.

Tears streamed down my cheeks as I confronted the depths of my fear. I was terrified of losing the connections I had begun to forge, terrified of the possibility that I might not be enough for the people I had come to care for. The darkness loomed larger than ever, a reminder that vulnerability often came hand in hand with the risk of heartbreak.

But as I wrote, I also began to recognize something profound. The fear I felt was a testament to the depth of my capacity to connect with others. It was a reminder that love and friendship were worth the risk, even if it meant facing the potential for loss. I couldn't allow my fear to dictate my choices any longer. I had taken the step toward healing, and I was determined to keep moving forward, even if it felt uncomfortable.

With a renewed sense of purpose, I closed my journal and took a deep breath, the tension in my chest beginning to ease. The road ahead would be filled with uncertainties, but I was ready to embrace it all—the laughter, the heartache, and the moments of connection that made life worth living.

The following morning, I awoke with a sense of clarity that had been elusive in recent days. I knew I needed to talk to the group about my feelings regarding Mia's departure. I couldn't allow my fears to fester in silence; I had to confront them head-on.

As we gathered for our morning meeting, I took a deep breath and spoke up. "I want to address what happened with Mia. Her leaving has hit me harder than I expected. I realized that I've been letting my fears dictate how I connect with all of you."

The room was silent, and I felt the weight of their attention upon me. "I've been terrified of losing the connections I've started to build. It feels like every time I let someone in, there's a chance they could walk away, and I don't know if I can handle that."

Sarah reached over, placing her hand on mine. "You're not alone in feeling that way. I think we all worry about losing what we're building here."

Tom nodded in agreement. "Yeah, it's scary to let people in. But isn't that what makes these connections so valuable? The risk of losing them only makes them more meaningful."

Their words resonated deeply within me, a gentle reminder that vulnerability was a double-edged sword—one that could cut deeply but also heal profoundly. In that moment, I felt a sense of relief wash over me. I wasn't alone in my fears; we were all navigating this journey together, each of us grappling with our own insecurities.

As we continued to share our thoughts, the atmosphere shifted. The conversations became more open, more authentic, a testament to the bonds we were forming. Together, we explored the intricacies of connection, loss, and the power of vulnerability.

With each word exchanged, I felt the layers of my own defenses begin to peel away. I realized that allowing myself to be vulnerable was not a weakness; it was an act of courage. The fear of loss would always be there, but so would the possibility of genuine connection.

As the session came to a close, I felt lighter, as if the weight of my fears had transformed into something more manageable. I had taken a step toward facing my truth, and in doing so, I had found solace in the shared experiences of others.

The days that followed were marked by a renewed sense of connection. We shared our stories, laughed at our quirks, and supported each other through moments of vulnerability. While the fear of loss still lingered, I began to embrace it as part of the journey rather than a barrier to my happiness.

One afternoon, as we gathered for a group activity, I felt a surge of gratitude for the connections I had forged. It was a reminder that even amidst the uncertainty, there was beauty in the shared experience of healing.

"Let's do something fun today," I suggested, my excitement bubbling to the surface. "How about a creative activity? We could make vision boards or something!"

The idea was met with enthusiasm, and soon the room was filled with laughter and the sounds of scissors cutting through paper. We shared our hopes and dreams as we crafted our boards, each image and word representing the vision we held for our futures.

As I pieced together my board, I felt a sense of purpose enveloping me. Each image I selected was a reflection of the life I wanted to build—a life filled with love, connection, and resilience. The shadows that had once loomed so large began to recede, replaced by the warmth of possibility.

In that moment, I realized that healing was not just about confronting the darkness; it was also about celebrating the light. I had taken a step toward embracing my truth, and in doing so, I had discovered the beauty of connection—a reminder that I was never truly alone.

As the day came to a close, I felt a renewed sense of hope bubbling within me. The journey ahead would undoubtedly be filled with challenges, but I was no longer defined by my fears. I was ready to embrace the fragments of truth that made up my story, each piece a testament to my resilience and capacity for connection.

With that thought in mind, I closed my eyes, allowing the warmth of hope to envelop me. Tomorrow would bring new opportunities for growth, and I was eager to chase the normal I had longed for, one step at a time.

Chapter 7: Facing the Abyss

The moment I stepped into the common area, I felt the weight of the day pressing down on me like a lead blanket. It wasn't just the walls closing in; it was the suffocating atmosphere of uncertainty that seemed to linger in the air, heavy and palpable. The usual chatter of my fellow patients faded into a dull hum as I settled into my usual spot in the corner. Today was different. Today, I felt a fissure in my carefully constructed façade.

Dr. Fredrickson had been relentless in our sessions lately. Each conversation felt like a strategic battle, with her probing questions uncovering layers of my psyche I had desperately tried to keep buried. I had managed to maintain control, steering the conversations away from the darker recesses of my mind, but I could feel the strain of the constant fight weighing on me. I was tired, and that fatigue seeped into every aspect of my being.

As I sat in the common area, my eyes scanned the room. A few patients were engaged in a game of cards, while others huddled together, exchanging quiet whispers. Laughter echoed from the far corner, but it felt distant and unreachable. I wondered what it would feel like to be part of that laughter, to genuinely connect with others instead of merely observing them from a distance.

"Hey, Elise," a voice called out, jolting me from my thoughts. It was Mia, a fellow patient with a vibrant personality that often contrasted with my own. She bounded over, her smile infectious, as if she could sense the shadows lurking behind my eyes.

"Hey," I replied, forcing a smile. "What's up?"

"Just finished a game. Want to join? We could use another player," she said, her enthusiasm brightening the dull atmosphere around us.

I hesitated, the familiar urge to retreat into solitude tugging at me. But the invitation lingered, an opportunity to connect, to step away from my thoughts, even if just for a moment. "Sure, why not?" I said, surprising myself.

As I joined the table, I was reminded of how much I craved connection, even if I had become adept at hiding from it. The game started, and for a brief while, I lost myself in the camaraderie, the laughter flowing around me like a lifeline. But deep down, I could feel the walls closing in, a storm brewing beneath the surface.

After a few rounds, I caught a glimpse of Dr. Hayes observing from the doorway. He stood there, arms crossed, watching me with an intensity that sent a shiver down my spine. I met his gaze, and for a fleeting moment, it felt as if he could see through the mask I wore. It unsettled me, making me acutely aware of my vulnerabilities.

"Everything okay?" Mia asked, her voice pulling me back into the present.

"Yeah, just..." I hesitated, unsure of how to articulate the turmoil within me. "Just tired, I guess."

Mia nodded, a knowing look in her eyes. "I get that. It's exhausting, all of this. But we're here for each other, right?"

I forced a nod, but the unease in my gut refused to dissipate. The laughter continued around me, but I felt detached, as if I were watching a scene unfold through glass. I tried to engage, but the more I tried, the more my mind drifted back to my session with Dr. Fredrickson.

"Let's take a break," I said suddenly, standing up. The others looked at me with mild confusion, but I didn't care. I needed air, space to breathe, to think.

I stepped outside into the courtyard, the crisp air hitting my face like a cold splash of water. The sky overhead was a brilliant blue, an unsettling contrast to the darkness swirling inside me. I leaned against the wall, closing my eyes and letting the sun warm my skin, grounding me in the moment.

But peace was fleeting.

The memories came crashing in, uninvited and relentless. The confrontation with my past, the regrets that clawed at my conscience, and the moments I had tried so hard to forget. I felt the weight of each one pressing down, a reminder of the battles I had fought and the ones still ahead.

"Are you okay?" The voice broke through the chaos. I opened my eyes to find Dr. Hayes standing a few feet away, his expression a mix of concern and curiosity.

"I'm fine," I replied, the words sounding hollow even to my ears.

He stepped closer, his gaze unwavering. "You don't look fine, Elise. I know you've been struggling."

I crossed my arms, the defensive gesture a reflex. "I'm just tired of talking about it, okay? I'm tired of pretending everything's fine when it's not."

His expression softened, the intensity in his eyes giving way to something more compassionate. "You don't have to pretend with me. You can let it out. I'm here to listen."

The sincerity in his voice broke through my defenses, and for a moment, I felt the walls crumbling around me. "What's the point?" I said, frustration bubbling beneath the surface. "I'm stuck in this place, and no matter how hard I try, it feels like I'm going in circles."

Dr. Hayes regarded me silently for a moment, his expression thoughtful. "You're not going in circles, Elise. You're moving forward, even if it doesn't feel that way right now. Healing isn't linear; it's messy and complicated. You have to allow yourself to feel those emotions, to face them head-on."

I wanted to scream, to push him away, but instead, I felt a flicker of understanding in his words. "And what if facing them is too much?" I whispered, my voice cracking.

"Then we take it one step at a time. You don't have to carry the weight of it all alone," he said gently.

His words struck a chord deep within me. I had spent so long isolating myself, pushing people away, convinced that I was stronger alone. But perhaps it was time to challenge that notion. I took a deep breath, feeling the air fill my lungs, and in that moment, I realized I had a choice.

"Okay," I said, my voice steadying. "Maybe I'm ready to talk about it. But I don't know where to start."

Dr. Hayes smiled, the warmth in his expression a balm to my frayed nerves. "Let's start with what's been weighing on your mind the most. Whatever feels right to you."

We settled onto a nearby bench, and as I spoke, the words poured out of me like a dam breaking. I shared my fears, the insecurities that clung to me like shadows, and the overwhelming sense of being lost in a world that seemed to have moved on without me.

"It's just... I feel like I'm in a constant battle," I admitted, my voice trembling. "I want to be better, but every time I take a step forward, I feel like I'm pushed back down."

Dr. Hayes listened intently, nodding in understanding. "That's a common experience for many people in recovery. You're not alone in this, Elise. It's okay to feel frustrated and overwhelmed. Acknowledge those feelings, but don't let them define you."

As we talked, I could feel the tension in my chest begin to ease. It was as if each word released a piece of the burden I had been carrying. I didn't have all the answers, and I still felt lost at times, but sharing my struggles with someone who truly understood made it feel a little less daunting.

"Thank you," I said quietly when I finally fell silent. "I didn't expect to feel so... relieved."

He smiled, the kindness in his gaze reflecting back at me. "That's the first step, Elise. Allowing yourself to be vulnerable. Healing begins when you let go of the need to be strong all the time."

We sat in comfortable silence for a moment, watching as the world moved around us. The courtyard felt different now, the atmosphere less suffocating and more hopeful. I could see the potential for connection in the laughter of my peers, the glimmers of understanding in their eyes.

"I think I want to try connecting with the others," I said suddenly, the thought surprising me. "I mean, really connecting."

"That's a great idea," Dr. Hayes encouraged, his expression brightening. "Building those connections can be incredibly beneficial for your healing process. It's about finding your tribe, the people who understand what you're going through."

I nodded, feeling a renewed sense of determination. It was time to take a leap of faith, to step outside my comfort zone and open myself up to the possibility of community.

As the day wore on, I returned to the common area with a different mindset. I approached the group playing cards and offered to join in again. To my surprise, they welcomed me without hesitation, pulling me into their conversations and laughter.

Mia flashed me a grin. "Glad to see you back, Elise! We were just about to start a new game."

The game unfolded, and I felt the warmth of their camaraderie wrap around me like a blanket. I allowed myself to laugh and engage, pushing past the remnants of my earlier unease. It was liberating, the way my heart lightened with each shared joke and playful jab.

But beneath the surface, I could still feel the echoes of my struggles. They were not gone; they had merely shifted, finding a new place in my consciousness. The fear that had gripped me earlier was still there, a constant companion, but I was beginning to understand that it didn't have to dictate my reality.

As the game progressed, I found myself sharing bits of my story with the others. I spoke about the challenges I faced, the moments of despair that had threatened to swallow me whole. And as I spoke, I saw their reactions—nodding heads, empathetic eyes, and soft smiles that conveyed understanding.

"I get it," one of the other patients said, a man named Jordan. "I've been there too. It's hard, but it helps to talk about it. It really does."

His words resonated with me, a reminder that I wasn't alone in this battle. We all carried our burdens, and while they were different, the weight of suffering united us.

In that moment, I felt a shift within me. It was subtle but powerful—a realization that I didn't have to hide my pain, that I could share it without fear of judgment. The connections I was building with my peers were grounding, a lifeline that tethered me to hope.

As the day turned into evening, we gathered around the communal dinner table. The chatter was lively, filled with stories and laughter. I looked around at the faces surrounding me—each one marked by their struggles, yet each one illuminated by the spark of resilience.

For the first time, I felt a sense of belonging, of being part of something greater than myself. And while the abyss still loomed in the background, I realized I didn't have to face it alone.

In the days that followed, I found myself opening up more during group sessions. I shared my thoughts and feelings, contributing to discussions in ways I hadn't before. The fear that had held me captive was slowly being dismantled, brick by brick, as I learned to embrace vulnerability.

With each passing day, I felt myself growing stronger, more resilient. I sought out my peers, engaging in activities together, and forming bonds that felt genuine and meaningful. We shared meals, played games, and supported each other in our individual journeys toward healing.

But the road was not without its bumps. There were days when the darkness threatened to creep back in, moments when I felt overwhelmed by the enormity of my emotions. During those times, I would retreat to the courtyard, seeking solace in the fresh air and sunlight.

It was on one of those afternoons that I encountered Mia again. She found me sitting alone, staring into the distance.

"Hey," she said softly, taking a seat beside me. "You doing okay?"

I sighed, rubbing my temples. "Some days are harder than others, you know?"

She nodded, her expression empathetic. "I get it. There are days when I feel like I'm back at square one. It's tough, but we've got to keep pushing through."

Her words resonated with me. "Yeah, I just... I want to keep moving forward. But sometimes it feels like I'm stuck."

Mia looked thoughtful for a moment before speaking. "You know what helps me? Finding little moments of joy in the day. It can be anything—a good book, a favorite song, or even just sitting outside and enjoying the sun. It's those small moments that remind us that healing is possible."

I considered her words, letting them sink in. "You're right. I need to focus on the positives, even if they're small."

We spent the rest of the afternoon talking about our favorite hobbies, our dreams, and the things that brought us joy. Mia's enthusiasm was infectious, and by the time we finished, I felt lighter, my heart buoyed by the conversation.

As the week progressed, I made a conscious effort to embrace those moments of joy. I found solace in painting, losing myself in colors and brushstrokes as I expressed my emotions on canvas. I discovered the therapeutic power of music, letting the melodies wash over me as I sang along, releasing pent-up emotions through lyrics.

I even took up journaling, pouring my thoughts onto the page in a stream of consciousness. Each entry felt like a release, a way to confront the chaos in my mind and transform it into something tangible. I filled the pages with my fears, my hopes, and the small victories I encountered along the way.

But as I grew stronger, a nagging sense of dread began to creep in. It was the impending end of the program—a date that loomed like a storm cloud on the horizon. The closer we got to graduation, the more I felt the anxiety bubble to the surface.

"Are you excited for graduation?" Mia asked one afternoon as we painted side by side.

"Honestly?" I replied, setting down my brush. "I'm terrified. What happens when we leave this place? I've made progress, but I'm afraid of what awaits outside these walls."

Mia nodded, her expression mirroring my concerns. "I think a lot of us feel that way. But remember, we've built a support network here. Just because we leave doesn't mean we have to go back to isolation."

Her words resonated with me, and I clung to the idea of connection. "You're right. Maybe we can stay in touch, form a group outside the program."

"That's a great idea!" Mia exclaimed. "We can be each other's lifelines. We're stronger together."

As the date approached, we began discussing plans for staying connected. We created a group chat, exchanged phone numbers, and made promises to meet regularly. The thought of maintaining those connections brought a sense of comfort, a reminder that I didn't have to face the world alone.

The day of graduation arrived, and the atmosphere was charged with a mix of anticipation and anxiety. I sat among my peers, feeling the weight of the moment settle heavily on my shoulders. Dr. Fredrickson stood before us, her voice steady and reassuring as she addressed our group.

"I'm incredibly proud of each and every one of you," she began. "You've faced your struggles head-on, and you've shown tremendous growth. Remember, this is not the end of your journey but the beginning of a new chapter."

Her words washed over me like a warm wave, and I felt tears prick at the corners of my eyes. It was a moment of recognition, of acknowledging the battles fought and the strength gained.

As we received our certificates, a sense of accomplishment surged through me. I had faced my demons, opened up to others, and taken steps toward healing. But as the ceremony concluded and we shared hugs and promises, a pang of fear clutched at my heart.

What lay ahead felt uncertain, like stepping into an abyss once more.

Later that evening, we gathered in the courtyard for a small farewell celebration. The air was filled with laughter and joy, but I couldn't shake the unease that settled deep within me. I watched my peers interact, their connections palpable and vibrant, while I felt like a fragile thread, ready to unravel.

As the night wore on, I took a moment to step away from the festivities, seeking solace in the quiet of the courtyard. I leaned against a wall, allowing the cool night air to calm my racing heart.

"Hey," a familiar voice broke through the silence. It was Dr. Hayes, his expression curious yet supportive.

"Just needed a breather," I admitted, my voice barely above a whisper.

He stepped closer, leaning against the wall beside me. "It's a big day. It's okay to feel overwhelmed."

"I'm scared," I confessed, my vulnerability spilling over. "I don't want to go back to being alone."

Dr. Hayes regarded me with understanding. "You're not alone, Elise. You have a community now. It won't be easy, but you've built connections that can carry you through."

I nodded, the weight of his words settling in. "I know. It's just... daunting."

"It is. But remember, healing is an ongoing journey. You'll face challenges, but you've also gained tools and support. Embrace it."

As we stood there in silence, the sounds of laughter fading into the background, I felt a flicker of hope ignite within me. It was the realization that while the path ahead was uncertain, I didn't have to walk it alone.

I took a deep breath, grounding myself in the moment. "Thank you for everything," I said, my voice steady. "For believing in me."

Dr. Hayes smiled, a genuine warmth radiating from him. "You've done the hard work, Elise. You should be proud of yourself."

As I returned to the celebration, the warmth of connection enveloped me once more. I embraced my peers, laughing and sharing stories, the weight of my fears lifted, if only for the moment.

The abyss still loomed in the distance, but I had found my footing. I had faced my fears, shared my struggles, and forged connections that grounded me in hope.

And as I stepped into the night, I carried with me the belief that I could face whatever lay ahead, not just as an individual but as part of a community that would support me through the shadows.

In the weeks that followed, I leaned into that belief. I stayed in touch with my peers, sharing updates, planning meetups, and continuing to open up about my journey. The support we offered one another became a lifeline, a reminder that healing wasn't a solitary endeavor.

I sought new experiences outside the confines of the program—hiking, attending workshops, and even volunteering at a local community center. Each step felt like a reclamation of my life, a way to build connections and find joy in the small moments.

But I also learned to honor the tough days. When the darkness crept in, I reached out to my peers, seeking comfort in their understanding. We created a rhythm of support, reminding one another that it was okay to stumble, that setbacks didn't erase our progress.

And in those moments of vulnerability, I discovered a newfound strength within myself. I was no longer defined by my past, but rather by the courage I found in facing it.

As I stood at the edge of the abyss, I realized it was not a void, but a space for growth. It was a reminder that even in the depths of struggle, there existed the potential for light.

And so, I took a deep breath, stepped forward, and embraced the journey ahead—a journey filled with uncertainty, yes, but also with hope, connection, and the strength to chase the normalcy I so desperately sought.

Chapter 8: Rebirth of the Self

The morning light filtered through my window, casting warm golden rays across the room. It was a new day, one that held the promise of change. As I stretched and took a moment to absorb my surroundings, I felt an unmistakable shift within me—a sense of readiness to embrace whatever life had in store.

The echoes of the program still resonated in my mind. Each lesson, each conversation had woven itself into the fabric of who I was becoming. Yet, I also felt the urge to explore beyond the familiar confines of what I had learned, to dig deeper into the layers of my existence that had long been buried beneath fear and doubt.

After breakfast, I decided to take a walk. The neighborhood surrounding my apartment had always seemed a little dull, but today, the air was crisp, and the world felt alive with possibilities. I stepped outside, allowing the sunlight to envelop me like a warm blanket. I hadn't truly appreciated this simple act of being outdoors in quite some time.

As I wandered, I noticed details I had previously overlooked—the vibrant flowers blooming in front of the houses, the laughter of children playing in the park, the couples strolling hand in hand. Each scene painted a picture of life, a reminder that there was beauty in everyday moments.

I made my way to the local coffee shop, a cozy spot I had discovered during my time in the program. The scent of freshly brewed coffee filled the air as I entered, the familiar chime of the doorbell signaling my arrival. I approached the counter, greeted by the barista with a warm smile.

"Hi there! The usual?" she asked, her voice bright.

"Actually, today I'll try something new," I replied, a wave of excitement washing over me. "Surprise me!"

Her eyes sparkled with delight as she prepared my drink. It felt freeing to embrace spontaneity, to allow myself to experience life without the constraints of anxiety.

With my drink in hand, I took a seat by the window. I pulled out my journal, the pages filled with thoughts, sketches, and fragments of my journey. As I sipped my coffee, I reflected on the transformation I had undergone.

The abyss, once a dark void that threatened to consume me, was now a space for growth. I had learned to navigate my fears, to confront the shadows without letting them dictate my reality. But there was still work to be done, layers to peel back, and fears to face.

After a while, I found myself lost in thought, jotting down ideas for a new project. Writing had become a form of therapy for me, a way to process my emotions and experiences. I felt inspired to write a series of essays reflecting on my journey—what I had learned, the friendships I had forged, and the resilience I had discovered within myself.

As I penned my thoughts, the door swung open, and a familiar face walked in. It was Mia, her presence instantly brightening the room. She spotted me and made her way over, her smile wide.

"Hey! Fancy seeing you here!" she exclaimed, taking a seat across from me. "What are you working on?"

"I'm actually starting a new writing project," I replied, excited to share. "I want to reflect on everything we experienced in the program—the highs and lows, the connections we made, and how it changed us."

Mia's eyes lit up. "That sounds incredible! You have such a gift for storytelling. I'd love to read it when you're done."

"I'd love that," I said, my heart swelling with gratitude. "It feels important to document this journey, to remind myself of how far I've come."

We chatted for a while, exchanging stories about our lives since graduation. Mia had started volunteering at a local mental health organization, using her experience to support others who were navigating their own struggles. Hearing her passion fueled my own determination to give back in some way.

"Have you thought about getting involved in the community?" she asked, sipping her drink. "There are so many opportunities to help others. I think it would be good for both of us."

"I have," I admitted. "I want to find a way to use my experiences to make a difference. It feels like a natural next step in this journey."

We brainstormed ideas, bouncing suggestions off one another until we settled on a plan. We would collaborate on a workshop for young adults struggling with mental health challenges, providing a safe space for them to share their stories and connect with others.

The idea ignited a fire within me. I envisioned a warm, inviting room filled with laughter, tears, and shared experiences—a space where vulnerability was embraced, and healing could begin. I felt a renewed sense of purpose, a desire to create something meaningful out of the darkness we had all faced.

Over the next few weeks, Mia and I poured our energy into planning the workshop. We designed activities that encouraged open dialogue, creative expression, and self-reflection. We reached out to local organizations, spreading the word and inviting individuals to join us in this transformative experience.

As the date of the workshop approached, a mix of excitement and anxiety bubbled within me. Would we be able to create the safe space we envisioned? Would people show up? Doubts crept in, but I reminded myself of the strength I had cultivated through my journey.

This was an opportunity to give back, to turn my experiences into something that could help others.

On the day of the workshop, I arrived early to set up the space. The room was filled with soft lighting, comfortable seating, and a few scattered art supplies. I took a deep breath, reminding myself that it was okay to feel nervous. This was part of the process—part of stepping outside my comfort zone.

As the participants began to arrive, I felt a surge of energy in the room. Faces both familiar and new filled the seats, each person carrying their own stories, their own burdens. Mia and I exchanged encouraging glances, silently reassuring one another as we welcomed everyone.

"Thank you all for being here today," I began, my voice steady despite the flutter of nerves in my stomach. "This is a space for us to connect, share, and support one another. We've all faced our own struggles, but together, we can create something beautiful."

The atmosphere felt electric, a palpable sense of hope permeating the air. We introduced ourselves, sharing snippets of our journeys, and as we did, I could see the barriers begin to dissolve. Laughter mingled with tears, and as the workshop progressed, it became clear that we were all there for one reason—to heal.

Mia led a guided art activity, encouraging everyone to express their feelings through colors and shapes. As I moved around the room, I witnessed the power of creativity in action. Participants poured their hearts onto canvas, each stroke a release, each color a reflection of their emotions.

After the art session, we gathered in a circle to share our creations. As individuals opened up about their experiences, I felt a deep sense of connection form among us. It was in those moments of vulnerability that healing truly began.

One woman spoke about her battle with anxiety, her voice trembling but resolute. "I often feel like I'm drowning in my thoughts, but being here today makes me realize I'm not alone. I can fight this."

Her words resonated with many in the room, igniting a wave of shared experiences. Others chimed in, recounting their own stories of struggle, resilience, and the hope that flickered within them.

As the workshop unfolded, I marveled at the bonds forming before my eyes. The group began to laugh, cry, and share in a way that felt organic and profound. In that space, we were no longer defined by our struggles but by the strength that emerged through our connection.

At the end of the day, we gathered once more to reflect on our time together. I felt an overwhelming sense of gratitude for each person who had shown up, for the courage it took to share their stories.

"Thank you all for being here today," I said, my voice thick with emotion. "Your willingness to open up and connect is what makes this journey worthwhile. We are not alone in this—together, we can support one another and find the light even in the darkest moments."

As the workshop came to a close, participants exchanged contact information, eager to stay connected. I watched with a heart full of hope as new friendships blossomed, each connection a testament to the power of vulnerability and shared experiences.

Mia and I shared a look of triumph as the last participant left the room. We had done it. We had created the safe space we envisioned, one that had allowed others to connect, heal, and grow.

In the weeks that followed, I received messages from many participants, thanking me for the workshop and sharing their progress. Some had started journaling, while others had found the courage to seek therapy or engage in creative pursuits.

The ripple effect of that day was profound, reminding me that change was possible, not just within ourselves but within our communities.

Feeling inspired, I continued to write, crafting essays that reflected my experiences and the stories I had encountered. I wanted to share the beauty of resilience, the power of connection, and the hope that could flourish even in the darkest of times.

One evening, as I sat in my favorite café, I noticed an open mic event happening in the corner. Intrigued, I decided to stay and listen. The atmosphere was buzzing with energy, and I felt a tug at my heart—a desire to share my own story.

As I watched individuals take the stage, baring their souls through poetry, music, and personal anecdotes, I felt a sense of camaraderie with each performer. I had spent so long hiding behind my fears, but now I craved the freedom of expression.

After a few acts, I decided to take a leap of faith. I approached the host and asked if I could share something. My heart raced as I stepped onto the small stage, the spotlight illuminating my nervous smile.

"Hi, everyone. My name is Alex, and I want to share a piece of my journey with you," I began, my voice shaking slightly. "I've been on a path of healing, and I believe that vulnerability can lead to profound connections."

As I spoke, I felt the warmth of the audience's energy. I shared snippets from my essays, weaving together themes of resilience, hope, and the importance of community. With each word, I felt the layers of my past shedding, revealing a version of myself that was stronger, more authentic.

When I finished, the room erupted in applause. I stepped down from the stage, feeling a rush of exhilaration and relief. I had taken a step toward embracing my truth, and it felt liberating.

In the months that followed, I continued to engage with the community. I hosted more workshops, participated in open mic events, and collaborated with local organizations focused on mental health advocacy. Each interaction reminded me of the beauty that emerged when we shared our stories.

Through this journey, I discovered the power of connection—how sharing our vulnerabilities creates a tapestry of understanding and empathy. The abyss I once feared had transformed into a space of growth and rebirth, allowing me to explore the depths of my being and emerge with newfound strength.

As I stood on the precipice of my next chapter, I reflected on the lessons learned and the bonds forged. I had turned my pain into purpose, my struggles into strength. I was no longer chasing normalcy; I was embracing the beautiful chaos of life.

The echoes of my past would always linger, but now, they served as reminders of how far I had come. With each step forward, I continued to embrace the journey ahead—one filled with uncertainty, yes, but also with hope, connection, and the courage to chase my own version of normal.

Chapter 9: The Weight of Choices

The morning sun streamed through my window, a gentle reminder of the fresh possibilities that awaited. As I prepared for the day, I couldn't shake the sense of anticipation brewing within me. There was a new opportunity on the horizon—one that could change the trajectory of my life.

After months of organizing workshops, sharing my story, and connecting with others, I had received an offer to speak at a local conference focused on mental health and wellness. The thought of standing on stage in front of a crowd filled me with both excitement and dread. It was a chance to reach a wider audience, to advocate for those who felt voiceless, and to share the lessons I had learned on my journey.

As I sipped my morning coffee, I reflected on the path that had led me here. The program had transformed me from a place of despair to a budding advocate for mental health. I had witnessed the impact of sharing stories, the way it forged connections and inspired healing. But this opportunity felt different; it carried a weight I hadn't fully grasped yet.

The conference was just a few weeks away, and the closer it got, the more my anxiety crept in. Would my message resonate with the audience? Would I be able to convey my experiences authentically? I made a promise to myself to prepare as best as I could, to channel my nerves into something productive.

I began to draft my speech, pouring my heart into the words. I wanted to emphasize the importance of vulnerability and the strength that comes from embracing our truths. I drew on the experiences I had shared in the workshops, the connections I had made, and the journeys of those who had opened up to me.

Days turned into weeks, and with each passing moment, I honed my message. I practiced in front of the mirror, rehearsed with friends, and recorded myself to analyze my delivery. The words became my mantra, a reminder of the significance of the message I was about to share.

The day of the conference arrived, and as I stood backstage, a wave of nervous energy coursed through me. The auditorium was buzzing with excitement, filled with individuals eager to learn and connect. I could hear the distant murmur of voices, the sound of chairs shifting, and the rustle of programs being opened.

A fellow speaker approached me, noticing my anxious demeanor. "You've got this," she said, her voice warm and encouraging. "Remember, you're not alone up there. We're all here for the same reason—to share and to learn from each other."

Her words were like a balm, soothing my nerves momentarily. I took a deep breath and closed my eyes, envisioning the impact I wanted to make. I reminded myself that I wasn't just speaking for myself; I was representing countless others who felt trapped in their own struggles.

When it was finally my turn to take the stage, I walked out with a mix of trepidation and determination. The spotlight enveloped me, and I felt the weight of every pair of eyes focused on me. I took a moment to absorb the atmosphere, the collective energy of hope and healing radiating from the audience.

"Hello, everyone," I began, my voice steady despite the flutter of nerves in my stomach. "My name is Alex, and today I want to talk about the power of choices—how the decisions we make shape our paths, our stories, and ultimately, our lives."

I shared my journey, recounting the pivotal moments that had led me to confront my fears and embrace vulnerability. I spoke about the workshops, the connections, and the healing that emerged from sharing our stories. Each word flowed from my heart, a testament to the transformation I had undergone.

As I spoke, I could see nods of recognition among the audience. Their eyes sparkled with understanding, and I felt an invisible thread connecting us all—a shared experience of struggle and resilience.

I emphasized the weight of choices, the impact they had on our mental health and well-being. "Every day, we are faced with decisions that shape our reality. We can choose to hide in the shadows of our fears, or we can step into the light of our truth. It's not always easy, but I promise you, it's worth it."

The audience listened intently, their rapt attention fueling my confidence. I shared stories of those I had met along the way—individuals who had chosen to embrace their struggles, who had turned pain into purpose. I highlighted the beauty of community, the way we could lift each other up and create spaces for healing.

As I reached the climax of my speech, I felt a surge of energy within me. "In a world that often tries to silence our voices, let us be the ones who speak up. Let us be the ones who share our stories, who embrace our truths. Together, we can create a tapestry of hope, a testament to the strength that resides in each of us."

The applause that followed was deafening. I stepped back from the microphone, overwhelmed with emotion. I had done it. I had shared my story, and in doing so, I had connected with others who were on their own journeys of healing.

After the presentation, I mingled with attendees, receiving messages of gratitude and encouragement. People approached me to share their stories, to thank me for being vulnerable. Each interaction reinforced the importance of connection—the way sharing our experiences can ignite hope in others.

As the day went on, I attended various workshops and panels, soaking up the knowledge and insights of other speakers. I felt invigorated, surrounded by a community of passionate individuals dedicated to mental health advocacy.

One workshop in particular stood out—a session on the power of storytelling in healing. The facilitator spoke about the importance of narrative, how the stories we tell shape our identities and influence our paths. I felt a resonance with every word, a reminder of the significance of sharing our truths.

After the session, I approached the facilitator. "I loved your talk! It really spoke to me. I've been working on my own narrative through writing and speaking."

She smiled, her eyes sparkling with enthusiasm. "That's wonderful! Storytelling is such a powerful tool. I encourage you to keep sharing your voice; it can create waves of change."

Inspired by her encouragement, I shared my vision for a storytelling project focused on mental health. I wanted to create a platform where individuals could share their experiences, a safe space for voices that often went unheard.

Her eyes widened with excitement. "I would love to help! Let's connect after the conference. I have some resources that could assist you in getting started."

The prospect of collaborating with someone so passionate about storytelling felt like a turning point. I exchanged contact information with her, eager to explore the potential of our partnership.

As the conference drew to a close, I reflected on the journey I had taken to get there. The fear and doubt that had once consumed me felt distant, replaced by a sense of purpose and connection. I had made choices that had led me to this moment, and each decision had been a step toward embracing my truth.

In the weeks following the conference, I stayed in touch with the facilitator, brainstorming ideas for the storytelling project. Together, we envisioned a series of workshops that would allow participants to explore their narratives and find empowerment through sharing.

The project quickly gained traction. We reached out to local organizations, securing partnerships that would provide support and resources. I felt a renewed sense of purpose as I poured my energy into this endeavor, excited to create a space for others to connect and heal.

As the first workshop approached, I found myself reflecting on the weight of choices once again. Every decision I had made, every risk I had taken, had led me to this moment—a chance to foster connection and healing in a community that desperately needed it.

On the day of the workshop, I arrived early to set up the space. The room was filled with warmth and light, inviting and comforting. I prepared materials, arranging chairs in a circle to encourage openness and dialogue.

As participants began to arrive, I felt a mix of excitement and nerves. Each person brought their own story, their own struggles, and I knew the power of sharing could transform the room into something sacred.

We introduced ourselves and shared what had brought us to the workshop. I was struck by the vulnerability present in the room; it felt as though we were all holding pieces of each other's hearts in our hands.

After some icebreaker activities, we delved into the heart of the workshop—exploring our narratives. I encouraged participants to reflect on their experiences, to consider the choices that had shaped their paths. Together, we created a safe space for sharing, where every voice was valued and every story mattered.

As the workshop progressed, I witnessed the magic of connection unfold. Individuals shared their struggles with anxiety, depression, and the weight of societal expectations. Tears flowed, laughter erupted, and a sense of camaraderie enveloped us.

One participant, Sarah, shared her story with raw honesty. "For so long, I felt like I was drowning in my thoughts. I didn't know how to articulate what I was feeling, and it left me isolated. But being here today makes me realize I'm not alone."

Her words resonated deeply, and soon others chimed in, sharing their own experiences of feeling trapped in their minds. The room buzzed with a collective understanding, a shared acknowledgment of the weight of mental health challenges.

As the workshop drew to a close, I facilitated a reflection session. Participants shared what they had learned, the connections they had formed, and the power of vulnerability in their lives.

"I feel lighter," one participant said, her eyes shining. "I've carried these stories alone for so long, and now I realize that sharing them is a form of healing."

With each reflection, I felt a swell of pride for what we had created together. We had opened doors to healing and connection, allowing individuals to embrace their narratives and find strength in vulnerability.

As the final moments of the workshop approached, I invited everyone to write down their takeaways and any commitments they wanted to make moving forward. I encouraged them to share their stories with others, to continue the cycle of connection beyond the workshop.

The room buzzed with energy as we shared our commitments aloud. It felt as though we had forged a pact—to support one another in our journeys, to carry the weight of each other's stories.

As the participants departed, I felt a profound sense of gratitude wash over me. The project had become more than just a workshop; it was a movement—a community dedicated to healing through storytelling.

In the months that followed, I continued to host workshops, each one filled with new faces and stories. I witnessed the transformative power of sharing unfold time and again, and my heart swelled with hope.

However, amidst the joy of these connections, I also felt the weight of my own journey. I was still navigating the complexities of my past, and while I had made significant strides, there were days when the shadows crept back in.

One particularly challenging week, I found myself spiraling into self-doubt. I questioned whether I was truly equipped to lead others on their paths when I was still grappling with my own. The pressure to be a beacon of hope felt overwhelming at times.

During one of our workshops, I confided in the group about my struggles. "I'm here sharing these stories with you, but I want to be honest—I still face my own challenges. There are days when I feel like I'm not enough, and I question my ability to help others."

The room fell silent, and I felt a wave of vulnerability wash over me. But instead of judgment, I was met with compassion. Participants began to share their own struggles with self-doubt and the challenges they faced, reminding me that we were all on this journey together.

One participant, Jake, spoke up. "We're all human. It's okay to have doubts. What matters is that we're here, supporting each other and learning together."

His words resonated deeply. In that moment, I realized that vulnerability wasn't a weakness; it was a bridge that connected us. We were all navigating the complexities of life, and sharing our struggles only strengthened the bonds we had forged.

As I continued to lead workshops and create spaces for connection, I learned to embrace my own journey. I discovered that it was okay to have moments of uncertainty and self-doubt. In fact, those moments only added depth to my understanding of resilience.

Through the storytelling project, I had become a part of a community that celebrated both the highs and lows of our journeys. We were each other's cheerleaders, lifting one another up as we navigated the often tumultuous waters of mental health.

As the year drew to a close, I reflected on the profound changes that had occurred. The weight of my past no longer felt like a burden;

instead, it was woven into the fabric of my story—a reminder of how far I had come.

I stood at the crossroads of my journey, contemplating what lay ahead. The choices I had made had led me to this point, and I felt a renewed sense of purpose. I envisioned expanding the storytelling project, reaching out to more communities and creating platforms for voices that often went unheard.

The echoes of my past served as both a reminder of my resilience and a motivator to keep pushing forward. I had turned my pain into purpose, and I was ready to embrace whatever came next.

In the following months, I began to lay the groundwork for a larger initiative—a community storytelling festival dedicated to mental health awareness. It would be a celebration of voices, an opportunity for individuals to share their stories in a supportive environment.

With each step I took, I felt the weight of choices—both past and present—transforming into a guiding light. I was no longer chasing normalcy; I was embracing the beautifully complex tapestry of life, woven together with the stories of those I had encountered along the way.

As the festival approached, I felt a surge of excitement and anticipation. I reached out to local artists, musicians, and mental health advocates, inviting them to participate in this celebration of storytelling. The community rallied behind the initiative, and I felt a sense of unity that reinforced the importance of connection.

On the day of the festival, the park was filled with laughter, music, and the sound of shared stories. I walked among the booths, soaking in the energy of the day. It was a vibrant celebration of resilience and hope—a testament to the power of storytelling.

As I stepped onto the stage for the closing remarks, I took a moment to breathe in the atmosphere. I could see familiar faces in the crowd—participants from my workshops, new friends I had made along the way, and supporters who believed in the mission.

"Thank you all for being here today," I began, my heart swelling with gratitude. "This festival is a testament to the power of our stories. Each of us has a narrative that deserves to be heard, and together, we can create a community of understanding and support."

As I spoke, I reflected on the journey that had led us here—the choices, the challenges, and the connections. I felt a sense of belonging, knowing that I was part of something greater than myself.

The festival ended with a collective release of balloons, each representing a story, a journey, or a hope. As the balloons floated into the sky, I couldn't help but smile, feeling the weight of choices transform into a lightness of being.

In that moment, I understood the significance of embracing our narratives. Each story, each choice, was a thread in the tapestry of our lives—a beautiful reminder of our resilience, our strength, and our capacity to heal together.

As I stood there, surrounded by a community of like-minded individuals, I felt ready to continue my journey—no longer chasing normal, but celebrating the beautiful, messy, and transformative experience of being human.

Chapter 10: Reflections in theAbyss

The world outside was vibrant with life, yet inside, I felt as though I was trapped in a dimly lit room, the walls closing in around me. My thoughts swirled like autumn leaves caught in a tempest—each one a reminder of the storms I had weathered. With the release of "Echoes of Resilience," I had gained the admiration of many, but it came at a cost. The deeper I ventured into my narrative, the more I unearthed unresolved emotions that lurked beneath the surface.

In the months following the anthology's publication, I had been invited to speak at various events, sharing the themes of resilience, vulnerability, and healing. It was a privilege, a way to connect with others who had similar stories. Yet, each time I stepped onto the stage, I felt a tightening in my chest—a reminder that while I was helping others, I was also grappling with my own truths.

One evening, as I prepared for yet another speaking engagement, I stood before the mirror, my reflection staring back at me with a blend of confidence and uncertainty. "Who are you really?" I whispered to my reflection, the question echoing in the empty room. The facade of strength was beginning to feel like a mask—one that concealed the fears and doubts I had yet to confront.

Despite the accolades and the warm applause, I was beginning to realize that the more I shared, the more I had to uncover. There were layers of my experience that remained unexamined, moments of darkness that still held power over me. It was time to embark on a deeper journey, to plunge into the abyss I had skirted around for too long.

With that resolve, I set out to explore the depths of my emotions. I turned back to my journal, a sacred space where I could lay bare my thoughts without judgment. I began to write about the shadows that lingered in the corners of my mind—the fears I had pushed aside in the pursuit of healing, the insecurities that whispered during quiet moments, and the unresolved grief that still haunted my heart.

As I wrote, I revisited the experiences that had shaped me—the moments that felt raw and unfinished. I reflected on the complexities of relationships—those that had nurtured me and those that had wounded me. The relationships with family members, friends, and even acquaintances had all played a role in my journey, and I realized it was essential to confront the emotions tied to each one.

I began with my father, a figure who had loomed large in my life, both as a source of strength and as a reminder of loss. I wrote about the days when he had been my hero, guiding me through childhood with unwavering support. But I also wrote about the pain of his absence—the years spent trying to bridge the emotional gap created by the divorce.

That night, I found myself sitting on the floor of my room, the weight of my thoughts pressing down on me. I took a deep breath, closed my eyes, and let the memories wash over me. I remembered the laughter we had shared, the adventures we had embarked upon, and the moments of quiet connection that had defined our relationship.

Yet, as the memories flooded back, so too did the unresolved anger—the feelings of betrayal when I learned that his new life had taken him further away from me. I had often masked this anger with understanding, convincing myself that he had done what was best for himself. But now, I allowed myself to feel the hurt, the loss of the father I had once known, and the emptiness that lingered in his absence.

In the following days, I decided to reach out to him. It had been years since we had spoken about our relationship, and I felt a growing urge to express my feelings, to articulate the wounds that had festered in silence. I sent him a message, inviting him to meet over coffee, hoping for an open conversation where we could both share our perspectives.

When we finally sat across from each other, I felt a mix of apprehension and hope. The café was filled with chatter, but our conversation felt like a world unto itself. I started slowly, recounting the fond memories of our time together—the fishing trips, the stories he told, and the lessons he imparted.

But as the conversation deepened, I couldn't hold back the truth any longer. "Dad," I said, my voice shaking slightly, "I need to talk about how your absence has affected me. I've spent years trying to understand it, and I think it's time we addressed it."

His expression shifted, a mix of surprise and vulnerability washing over him. "I never intended to hurt you," he said quietly. "I thought I was doing what was best for everyone, but I see now how my decisions impacted you."

We spent hours in that café, navigating the complexities of our relationship. It was a painful yet liberating experience, one that allowed us both to articulate our feelings, to acknowledge the wounds we had carried for so long. I felt lighter as we spoke, as though a weight had been lifted from my heart.

The following week, I turned my attention to another relationship that had left its mark on me—my best friend from college, Rachel. She had been a pillar of support during my struggles, yet our friendship had also been tested by misunderstandings and unspoken words.

I arranged to meet Rachel at our favorite park, the place where we had shared laughter and tears during our university years. As we walked along the path, I felt the familiar warmth of nostalgia, but also a sense of trepidation.

"Rachel," I began, glancing at her as we strolled. "There's something I've been wanting to talk about. I've felt this distance between us lately, and I think it's time we address it."

She paused, her brow furrowing slightly. "I've felt it too," she admitted, her voice laced with vulnerability. "It's like we've both been holding back."

We found a bench beneath the shade of a large oak tree and settled in. As we spoke, I laid bare my feelings of inadequacy, my fears of being a burden to her. I expressed how I had often felt like I was in her shadow, struggling to measure up to her success and strength.

Rachel listened intently, her eyes softening with understanding. "You're not a burden to me," she said, her voice steady. "I admire your resilience, and I want you to know that you're not alone in this. I've faced my own struggles, and I think we both need to be more open with each other."

As we shared our vulnerabilities, I felt the barriers between us begin to dissolve. We spoke about our fears, our aspirations, and the challenges that had shaped our paths. It was a cathartic experience, one that deepened our connection and reminded us of the power of honesty in friendship.

With each conversation, I began to unravel the threads of my past, weaving them together into a narrative that was both honest and healing. I found solace in the act of vulnerability, recognizing that sharing my truth allowed others to do the same.

However, even as I navigated these relationships, I was still haunted by memories of my childhood. I decided it was time to confront the remnants of those formative years, to reflect on the moments that had shaped my identity.

I returned to my childhood home, a place filled with echoes of laughter and shadows of sorrow. As I walked through the familiar rooms, I felt a mixture of nostalgia and grief. I paused in front of the old tree in the backyard, the one where I had spent countless hours climbing and dreaming.

Sitting beneath its branches, I closed my eyes and let the memories flood back. I recalled the innocence of my childhood, the moments of joy that had filled my days. But alongside those memories came the challenges—the isolation I had felt during my teenage years, the longing for connection that often went unfulfilled.

I began to write about these experiences, allowing the words to flow freely. I wrote about the friendships that had slipped through my fingers, the moments when I had felt invisible, and the longing for acceptance that had driven me to wear a mask of confidence.

As I penned these reflections, I felt a sense of liberation. I recognized that the journey of healing was not just about acknowledging the pain; it was also about celebrating the strength that had emerged from those struggles. I was not defined by my past but rather shaped by my ability to navigate through it.

In the following weeks, I poured my heart into this new chapter of my writing, crafting narratives that intertwined my experiences with those of others. I reached out to friends who had also faced challenges and invited them to share their stories with me. Each conversation was a reminder that we were not alone in our struggles; we were part of a larger tapestry of shared experiences.

As I wove these stories together, I began to see the beauty in the complexity of life. Each narrative was a thread, contributing to a larger tapestry that celebrated resilience, vulnerability, and the human spirit's capacity for growth. I titled this new project "Reflections in the Abyss," a nod to the depths we often fear yet must confront to emerge stronger.

One afternoon, I organized a small gathering at my home, inviting those who had shared their stories with me. I wanted to create a space where we could celebrate our journeys and the connections we had forged. As my friends arrived, I felt a wave of excitement mixed with nervousness.

The atmosphere was filled with warmth and laughter as we shared snacks and stories. I listened intently as each person recounted their journey, their struggles and triumphs weaving together like a beautiful melody. The power of shared experiences resonated deeply within me, reminding me of the strength found in vulnerability.

After everyone had shared, I stood up, my heart swelling with gratitude. "Thank you all for being here," I said, my voice shaking slightly. "I want to honor each of your stories. They remind us that while we may have faced our own struggles, we are not alone in this journey."

We spent the evening discussing the importance of storytelling and connection, exploring the ways our experiences intertwined. Each laugh, tear, and moment of silence felt sacred—a testament to the power of shared humanity.

As the gathering came to a close, I felt a profound sense of fulfillment. I realized that the process of exploring my past had not only deepened my understanding of myself but had also forged connections with others who shared similar experiences. We were all navigating our own abysses, yet together, we were finding light in the darkness.

In the weeks that followed, I dedicated myself to refining "Reflections in the Abyss." The writing flowed effortlessly, and with each page, I felt more connected to my truth. I wanted this project to serve as a beacon of hope, a reminder that even in the depths of despair, there is a path toward healing and connection.

As I sat at my desk late one night, surrounded by the gentle hum of my thoughts, I felt a sense of clarity. The echoes of my past had transformed into a chorus of resilience—a reminder that the journey of healing is not linear but rather a beautiful, messy tapestry of experiences.

I reached for my journal, my trusted companion, and began to pen a letter to my future self. In it, I wrote about the lessons I had learned, the importance of embracing vulnerability, and the strength that comes from confronting one's fears. I wanted to remind myself that it was okay to lean into the discomfort, to acknowledge the shadows that lingered, and to seek connection amidst the chaos.

As I finished the letter, I felt a sense of peace wash over me. The journey of "Reflections in the Abyss" had become a path of healing, not just for myself but for all those who dared to confront their own stories. I understood that we are all part of something greater—a collective narrative that weaves together the threads of our shared humanity.

With renewed purpose, I committed to sharing this project with the world. I reached out to publishers, eager to bring "Reflections in the Abyss" to life. The process of refining my work felt invigorating, a testament to the growth I had experienced on this journey.

As the publication date approached, I felt a blend of excitement and apprehension. I knew that sharing these intimate stories would expose my vulnerabilities, but I also understood that this was part of the healing process.

On the night of the book launch, I stood in front of a crowd of familiar and unfamiliar faces, my heart racing with anticipation. I took a deep breath, reminding myself of the journey that had led me here—the connections forged, the stories shared, and the strength found in vulnerability.

As I spoke, I felt the weight of my words resonate with the audience. I shared not only the themes of the book but also the significance of connection and resilience. Each person in that room was a part of the tapestry I had woven, each story a thread contributing to the larger narrative of healing.

When the evening concluded, I was met with warm applause and heartfelt conversations. Many attendees approached me, sharing their own stories, their own reflections on resilience. In that moment, I felt an overwhelming sense of gratitude—a reminder that the journey of healing is never solitary; it is shared among us all.

As I left the venue that night, I looked up at the stars twinkling in the sky, feeling a sense of belonging amidst the vastness of the universe. I understood that the echoes of my past had guided me toward this moment—a moment of connection, healing, and celebration of the human spirit.

"Reflections in the Abyss" became more than just a book; it transformed into a movement—a call to embrace vulnerability, share our stories, and uplift one another. And as I continued on this journey, I carried with me the echoes of resilience, illuminating the path ahead.

I knew that while the journey was far from over, I was ready to embrace the beautifully messy nature of life with open arms. The abyss, once a place of fear, had become a source of strength, a reminder that within the depths of our struggles lies the potential for profound growth and connection.

THE END

The edits and layout of this print version are Copyright © 2024 By Jessica Hintz

Milton Keynes UK
Ingram Content Group UK Ltd.
UKHW040840021124
450589UK00001B/152